MASTER OF THE GAME

"You lied to me when you said you could play chess," Hawkhurst accused Christine.

"Never," Christine responded. "You asked me if I should like to play chess with you. I answered yes, as I would very much like to. You never asked if I knew the game."

Hawkhurst rose, his great height towering above her rested form. He brought a chess board and pieces and set it between them.

"You—you're willing to teach me?" Christine said.

He smiled and a shiver ran through her. "I should like to teach you many things, Christine. Chess is only the beginning . . . ."

MICHELLE KASEY is the pseudonym of Kasey Michaels, which is the pseudonym of Kathie Seidick, a surburban Pennsylvania native who is also a full-time wife and the mother of four children. Her love of romance, humor, and history combine to make Regency novels her natural medium.

Moonlight Masquerade

by

Michelle Kasey

A SIGNET BOOK

NEW AMERICAN LIBRARY

PUBLISHED BY
PENGUIN BOOKS CANADA LIMITED

NAL BOOKS ARE AVAILABLE AT QUANTITY DISCOUNTS WHEN USED TO
PROMOTE PRODUCTS OR SERVICES. FOR INFORMATION PLEASE WRITE TO
PREMIUM MARKETING DIVISION, NEW AMERICAN LIBRARY,
1633 BROADWAY, NEW YORK, NEW YORK 10019.

First Printing, August, 1989

2   3   4   5   6   7   8   9

SIGNET TRADEMARK REG. U.S PAT OFF AND FOREIGN COUNTRIES
REGISTERED TRADEMARK — MARCA REGISTRADA
HECHO EN WINNIPEG, CANADA

SIGNET, SIGNET CLASSIC, MENTOR, ONYX, PLUME,
MERIDIAN and NAL BOOKS are published in Canada by Penguin
Books Canada Limited, 2801 John Street, Markham, Ontario,
L3R 1B4
PRINTED IN CANADA
COVER PRINTED IN U.S.A.

To my son, Eddie, who can see the good inside,
and always takes the time to look

ONE

The English Countryside, 1814

"Oh, we're going to die, we're going to die. I just know we're going to die!"

Christine Denham hung tightly onto the coach strap—and her temper—as she listened to her beloved but exasperating aunt recite this singsong litany of doom and disaster. Wasn't it enough that the constant jolting of the coach was rapidly making her rue her choice of rabbit stew for luncheon? As a matter of fact, considering the way she felt now, she just might not ever eat again.

"We're not going to die, Aunt Nellis," she assured the older woman through gritted teeth.

"A fine lot you know, Christine," Aunt Nellis retorted, reaching up to clamp her feathered hat more firmly to her head. "I've traveled before—to Bath, when I was your age. It was a most pleasant excursion, both coming and going. This is quite different, I assure you. I know disaster when I look it in the eye."

Christine had heard about Aunt Nellis's trip to Bath numberless times and knew that it had taken place in June, when snow was as scarce as hen's teeth, but she didn't feel it necessary to point this out. "You were the one who wanted to get to town early in order to have everything ready for the Season," she could not resist saying. "Besides, I'm sure the coachman wouldn't have said we could continue the journey after luncheon if there was any great danger. He travels this route all the time."

Aunt Nellis widened her slightly protuberant hazel eyes and shakily pointed to the scene outside the off-window. "No danger? No danger? It has been snowing like this for the past three hours, Christine. Snowing so heavily that I cannot even see the trees as we pass by them. And you say there is no danger? What would constitute danger to you, Christine? An avalanche?"

Shrugging, Christine smiled, trying to put a brave face on things. "At least now you won't have to worry about all those highwaymen you told me were waiting for us to come along, giving them two nice white throats to slit. I'm sure they're all sitting quite happily in their little thieves' warrens, their bare toes pointed toward the fire, telling each other whooping lies about the money and jewels they have taken from honest folk like us."

Aunt Nellis sniffed her disdain and lifted her head a fraction, forgetting that the movement would accentuate the beaklike appearance of her thin nose and give her niece an unimpeded look at the double chin she usually tried so hard to conceal. "Don't be impertinent, Christine," she said haughtily, pulling up the canvas shade to block the distressing vision of falling snow. "Gentleman don't like impertinent young ladies."

"Then, dear aunt, I suggest you immediately tug on that rope and order the coachman to turn this equipage about for our return to Manderley, for my debut is bound to be a dismal disappointment to you. You see, I find I have a definite attachment to impertinence."

Nellis Denham shook her graying head. "Hush, child. If your poor departed father heard you he would simply perish from the pain of your ingratitude," she declared feelingly, her garbled statement causing her niece to bite hard on her inner lip to keep from laughing aloud. "He so wanted you to go to London and be a success."

"Papa *perished* when I was two years old, Aunt Nellis," Christine stated, "chasing after Mama because she ran away with Mrs. Warburton's wastrel brother. I doubt he took the time to relate the many detailed instructions and hopes for my future you have quoted all these years before he mounted his horse and rode off into the night."

"Christine!" Aunt Nellis pressed a hand to her mouth and slowly counted to ten. The child was breaking her heart; absolutely breaking her heart! "Well, he did too," she said at last, knowing her niece was right but refusing to acknowledge it. "He distinctly told me he wanted you to go to London for a Season."

"And he—also before charging off after his naughty wife—told you that I was forbidden to ever ride horses, and I was to sew a fine seam, and

I was to never leave my fork propped drunkenly on the edge of my plate, and I was forbidden to cross my legs, even at the ankle, and I was never, *ever* to allow any man to—"

"Enough, Christine!"

Christine reached across the coach to lay her free hand on her aunt's arm. "I'm sorry, dearest," she said sincerely, as she had only been hoping to draw the woman's mind away from the storm raging outside. "But don't you see? I know that it was you who raised me, you who wants me to have this Season. You love me, Aunt Nellis. You love me, and I love you. You don't have to hide your hopes for me behind the father I don't remember. Now, why don't *you* ask me not to be impertinent and see what happens?"

Nellis looked at her niece in silence for a long time as the rising wind howled outside the coach, then slowly nodded. "We'll probably freeze to death in this awful coach before we ever reach London anyway," she groused halfheartedly, summoning a weak smile.

Christine gave up her attempt to sidetrack her aunt from her usual pessimistic thoughts—for after all, they seemed to bring her so much joy—and agreed: "The coachman will probably hop down off his perch once we're in front of the town house you rented on Half Moon Street and pull open the door, just to have the two of us topple out onto the cobblestones like huge blocks of ice. Why, they'll have to wait until we thaw in order to bury us."

Her niece's words conjured up a mental picture

that, while depressing, turned Aunt Nellis's mind to the problems involved with such an occurrence. She was always happiest while planning strategies for dealing with disaster. "Our knees will be rigidly bent, of course, because we're seated. We couldn't fit very neatly in a coffin that way, could we? How embarrassing! Do you suppose we should tie a few ribbons about our skirts at our ankles? Just so that we don't show too much leg as we topple?"

Christine was saved from answering as the coachman drew the horses to a stop and opened the trapdoor that looked down into the interior of the hired coach. "It's snowin' pretty awful, ladies, an' it be more 'an five miles to the nearest postin' house. We ain't goin' ta make it iffen I doesn't spring 'em as much as I can in this bloodly—er, that is ta say, in this bad storm. Yer'll have ta hold on, ma'am, miss. It's bound ta be a bumpy ride."

Before the trapdoor had slammed shut once more Aunt Nellis was already well launched into her second chorus of, "Oh, we're going to die, we're going to die. I just know we're going to die!"

Holding onto the strap with both hands, Christine, her queasy stomach forgotten, did her best to console her distraught aunt, who now appeared to be a most creditable prophetess of doom. The coach was swaying violently as it moved along the highway, its wheels sliding rather than rolling over the packed snow and ice.

Forgotten also was the fact that her toes were freezing, or the knowledge that she was heading toward London and the Season she hadn't wanted in the first place. All Christine could think of at the moment was keeping her aunt calm. That, and trying very hard not to panic herself.

Deciding to investigate—just to double-check the coachman's assertions—she rolled down a window to look outside, only to have her cheeks viciously stung by the sleet that was now pelting the countryside. It was only three o'clock but it was as dark as midnight.

The coach slowed to a crawl as the weary horses worked to haul their passengers and a small mountain of baggage up a steep incline and Christine called out to the coachman, warning him to remember that what goes up must eventually come down, and there could be a dangerous descent waiting for them. Her words were snatched away by the wind just before Aunt Nellis, grabbing her niece most inelegantly about the waist, hauled her back inside.

"Whew! It looks like the end of the world out there," Christine said as she collapsed against the seat. Looking at her aunt's ashen face, she quickly regretted her thoughtless words. "Oh, Aunt, I'm so sorry," she began, letting go of the strap to reach out her hands in comfort, "I didn't really mean it actually is the—*oh*!"

The howling wind had turned the road at the crest of the hill into a mass of deep, treacherous frozen ruts. The off-leader stumbled, regained its balance, then stumbled once more, this time losing its footing completely. One moment the horses were straining to move forward, and the next moment they were wild-eyed, plunging and twisting in their efforts to avoid the fallen horse.

The coachman employed his whip, desperately trying to restore order, but to no avail. Within the space of a heartbeat, control of the coach shifted from the driver to the team, and lastly to the elements. The panicked horses drove forward against the shaft, their shod hooves finding no purchase on the roadway as the coach, now on the descent, gathered force behind it.

Aunt Nellis screamed again and again as they tipped first one way, then the other as she vainly tried to grasp at Christine's helplessly tumbling body. She heard the fatal sound of the shaft breaking away from the body of the equipage just before the coach gave a sickening lurch and the whole world turned upside down.

TWO

Hawk's Roost

*I*t was the very devil of a night outside, fit for neither man nor beast. Lord Hawkhurst was seated in his private study as was his custom each evening after dinner during clement or inclement weather, a book in his lap and a snifter of warmed, aged brandy at his side.

The howling wind suited the earl's frame of mind. In fact, he might, if this melancholy mood stayed with him, take a walk in the windswept garden before retiring to his chamber for the night.

He closed his eyes, mentally picturing himself standing at the crest of the small cliff at the end of the garden path, his uncovered head thrown back, challenging the elements. He would face into the wind and feel the power of nature assaulting his body, whipping at his face, tearing at his straining muscles. If he could stand there, just so, for a quarter of an hour, if he could conquer the wind and the cold for that precise space of time, then he would reward himself by sending Lazarus to London to purchase him a—

He closed the book, his short curse echoing through the room. Was this what he had come to? Playing childish games to fill the empty hours? And what, he asked himself, would he have Lazarus buy that he did not already possess?

He had enough paintings and silver and fine, handcrafted furniture. He had expensive silks and custom-tailored clothing—enough to outfit a small army. He had wines and delicate cheeses, the finest chef, the most loyal servants—everything a man could possibly ask for and more.

There was nothing, not a single thing, the Earl of Hawkhurst lacked.

He reached out a hand to cradle the brandy snifter in his palm. It was a truly lovely piece. Perfect, actually, except for one small air bubble that was barely noticeable except to someone with a discerning eye. His long, thin fingers caressed the delicate glass bowl as he brought it to his lips. He drank deeply, savoring the taste, then flung the flawed snifter into the fireplace. The flames caught at the brandy, flaring briefly, and then all was quiet once more except for the lonely howling of the wind.

An hour passed, an hour during which the earl sat sprawled inelegantly in his deep leather chair, his long, booted legs flung out in front of him as he glared at the ever-changing faces in the fire, before a noise in the hallway roused him from his brown study. Someone was knocking on the front door of Hawk's Roost.

"No," Hawkhurst mused aloud, "someone is trying their utmost to break down the front door." Was he not to be allowed any peace, even in the midst of a storm? Who dared to intrude on his misery? "Lazarus, damn you!" he shouted above the sound of something heavy hitting the thick wooden door. "Put a stop to that infernal racket!"

The earl heard footsteps in the hallway, followed by a gentle rapping on his study door. "Enter!" he allowed imperiously.

"Excuse me, your lordship, but it appears there's been an accident on the road. There are three travelers without, begging shelter for the night."

Hawkhurst sat forward so that his right profile was visible in front of the deep wingback of his chair. Shifting his gaze so that one piercing green eye impaled the servant standing just inside the door, he said, "And what, pray tell, dear Lazarus, does that have to do with me? Only fools would travel in this weather. There is no room at Hawk's Roost for more fools. I am here. One fool is sufficient."

The servant bobbed his head up and down several times, swallowing so hard that his Adam's apple popped out from beneath his starched collar. "Yes, your lordship, of course," he agreed, adding, "only, you see, sir, it's a coachman and two ladies."

"Ladies, my good Lazarus? Are you quite sure?"

"Yes, your lordship, two of them, actually. The younger one's hurt pretty bad, I think. The old one's wringing her hands and moaning to beat the Dutch, too. She says it's been hours since their coach overturned and they're all about to freeze solid. And something about coffins, sir, but I'm afraid I didn't quite catch it."

Hawkhurst pinched the bridge of his nose between his thumb and forefinger. "This tale you're relating sounds intriguing, to say the least, but it's not my problem. Obviously the injured one requires the services of a doctor. Do I look like a doctor, Lazarus?"

"No, your lordship."

"Then, dear man, may I make a suggestion? Why not have my coach brought around and transport the ladies to the village? That shouldn't prove to be an insurmountable problem. Then see that I am brought another snifter. It would appear the first one suffered an accident."

Lazarus had been with the earl long enough to know when to fight and when to withdraw. Clearly it was time for the latter. "Yes, your lordship," he said, bowing himself out of the room. "Your carriage. The village. I'll see to it immediately, your lordship."

"You're a good man, Lazarus," the earl complimented softly, settling back into the shadows. "The best of my inheritance."

Unfortunately, even the best of Hawkhurst's inheritance was no match for the woman standing just inside the great wooden door of his domicile. "Turn us away? Turn us away!" the earl heard a high, shrill voice shriek. "With my baby all but dead, you would turn us away? Not while there's breath left in my body, sirrah! I'll not move one inch from this spot until I have seen your master!"

Hawkhurst propped an elbow on the arm of the

chair and dropped his chin in his hand, one eye watching the door, waiting for Lazarus's return, which was not long in coming. "Er, your lordship—" the servant began, his voice quavering.

"Yes, Lazarus," the earl said, cutting him off. "I heard. It seems our unwanted visitor is a most formidable, if dramatic, woman. Well, I can't have her upsetting you, can I, Lazarus? I value you too highly. Very well. Bring me my cloak, if you please," he commanded, rising from the chair to face the servant.

Lazarus hastened to do his master's bidding, fetching the hooded black silk cloak from a nearby chair and then helping the earl don it, easing the material over the man's left arm and then standing on a stool to carefully place the hood over Hawkhurst's coal-black head, so that his lordship's face was thrown into shadow.

"Thank you, Lazarus," Hawkhurst said, already moving toward the study door, his strides long and purposeful. "Shall we join the ladies?"

The earl stepped into the wide black and white tiled foyer, tugging his hood further down over his head as he cursed the extra candles some idiot had deemed fit to light due to the arrival of their nocturnal visitors. There were three people waiting for him, although his only clear view was of a tall, exceedingly homely, exceptionally angry older woman who looked fully capable of sitting herself down in the middle of the room, refusing to be moved.

"Madam," Hawkhurst said quietly in his deep voice, bowing in the woman's direction. "I believe you requested my appearance."

Nellis Denham had just then been concentrating on whether or not her niece's small chest was still moving and giving serious consideration to taking the small hand mirror from her reticule to place it at Christine's mouth—just to be sure she was breathing—but at the sound of the earl's voice she swung fully about, and saw her unwilling host for the first time.

What she saw immediately drove all thoughts of berating the man for his ill manners straight from her mind. Her prominent eyes widened until they showed white all around their hazel centers as her gaze took in the strange sight in front of her.

The man was tall, exceedingly tall, and quite thin, or at least he seemed thin beneath the enveloping black cloak that swirled about his knees as he came to a halt more than ten feet away from her. He was clothed all in black, with only the snowy white of one shirt cuff, his perfectly tied cravat, and the flesh tone of his right hand to serve as contrast. The hand was raised, holding onto the tip of the hood like a villager tugging at his forelock.

His appearance was a shock, there was no disguising it, but Nellis Denham was made of extremely strong stuff. Lifting her chin a fraction, she returned defiantly, "Indeed, yes, my lord, I did. In fact, I demanded it! I have a question for you. How dare you deny us shelter?"

"Quite easily, madam," Hawkhurst replied, about to turn away. "I did not ask you here."

"You would let my niece die?" Nellis challenged, stepping away from the coachman, who was still holding the unconscious girl, and giving the earl a clear vision of his third unwanted guest.

Christine Denham's body resembled that of a child's rag doll, lying limp and helpless in the arms of the strapping coachman, her legs dangling over one broad forearm, her hands curled limply in her lap, her head, covered by her cloak, resting against his broad chest.

"A child?" Hawkhurst questioned, for the coachman was very big and Christine appeared to be very small. He turned to Lazarus, his voice ringed with anger. "You didn't tell me it was a child."

Nellis quickly grasped at the straw the earl had inadvertently handed her. "The only child of my dear, departed brother, and the one joy of my life," she pleaded hastily. "Please, my lord, you cannot send us back out into the storm. You cannot let her die!"

Lazarus opened his mouth, about to say something, then appeared to think better of it and merely nodded before leading the way to the stairs. "If you'll follow me, please, ma'am," he said, not daring to look at his master, "I'll show you to your rooms."

Hawkhurst watched the small party ascend the staircase, then returned to his study, removing the silk cloak with his right hand and flinging it to the floor. He walked over to the hearth to stand staring down into the fire. "A child," he said aloud, closing his eyes. "What in bloody hell am I going to do with a child?"

THREE

*I*t was dark in the second-best bedchamber Hawk's Roost had to offer, dark except for the soft yellow circles of light cast by the flickering fire and one small bedside candle. The woman Lazarus had identified as one Miss Nellis Denham was slumped in an overstuffed chair in the corner, her lady-like snores assuring him that she had at last succumbed to her fatigue.

Hawkhurst approached the bed on silent feet. It was a large bed, over a hundred years old, its users forced to gain its comfort by way of a set of wooden stairs. The person occupying the bed, however, was small. Very small, and very still.

The earl moved closer to the head of the bed to look down on his unwanted visitor, the niece, Christine Denham. He inhaled sharply, disbelievingly, angrily. He had been tricked! This was no child!

Her ebony hair, spreading outward from a slight widow's peak, was splayed across the pillows; long, thick, and lustrous. It constrasted sharply with the pallor of her small, heart-shaped face. Accentuating her paleness were her black winglike brows and the thick, sooty lashes that shadowed her cheeks.

There was a hint of blue tinging her closed eyelids, not caused by bruising, but a result of her fair, nearly transparent skin. Her face was made up of gentle curves, her small, straight nose and soft, pouting lips balanced by a short but strong chin that boasted both a slight point at its tip and a shallow cleft.

His gaze traveled downward, past the slim neck to the high closing of her modest nightgown, an ancient piece unearthed from only the good Lord knew where. There wasn't much of her, her toes lifting the blanket little more than five feet below the tip of her head, but the slight outline was definitely not that of a child. And her hands, lying at her sides atop the blanket, were beautifully formed, with long, tapering fingers and short-cut oval nails.

Christine Denham was a woman of quality, a very beautiful woman. It had been so long, an eternity, since he had been in the presence of a refined woman. His first thought was one of escape, fearing that she should wake and find him here, all but drooling over her. But she was unaware of him, unconscious. What was the harm of lingering a few moments more?

After several minutes spent staring at the still form he forgot himself sufficiently to lean closer, the better to see her in the dim candlelight. She appeared to be asleep, with no sign of injury anywhere, but the earl already knew that she had sustained a sharp blow to the back of her head as the rented traveling coach she had been riding in had overturned on the side of a hill.

She'd been unconscious now for over two hours, a circumstance that had caused Lazarus to come to his master and voice his concern. It was to satisfy his servant's uneasiness that the earl had agreed to come to the bedchamber at all.

Snow clogged the road to the village so there was no medical help available, not that the earl put much stock in doctors, but now he wished there were some way to summon a physician. His unexpected guest looked so fragile, so completely vulnerable, and Hawkhurst couldn't remember the last time he had felt so helpless, so useless.

No, that wasn't true. He could remember such a time, and did, closing his eyes against the pain he knew would follow his thoughts. But this time he didn't allow himself the luxury of melancholy. This time perhaps it wasn't too late to help. The girl was still alive, and while there was life there was hope.

Involuntarily, almost without thought, he reached out his right hand and took hold of hers. Her hand was limp, and very cold, and he squeezed it tightly, willing his own considerable strength into her small body. Concentrating his gaze on her beautiful pale face, he spoke softly, murmuring comforting sounds that he hoped would somehow ease her dreams.

He told her all about his childhood in nearby Surrey, and the little hidden glen he had chosen as his favorite thinking place. He spoke of gently rolling hills, and fragrant summer flowers—a place where a person could go when in trouble and always count on coming away feeling refreshed, renewed. Strengthened. He bade her to travel in her mind to that pleasant glen, and allow the beauty of the place to soothe her weary body.

How long he stood there he did not know. He was oblivious to the passage of time, uncaring of his own physical discomfort, the slow throbbing that began in his left shoulder and spread down his arm. He was accustomed to spending his nights awake, preferring the cloak of darkness to the cloak he was forced to wear in the daylight.

Finally, as the fire began to die in the grate, Christine moved slightly in the bed, her hand closing tightly about his even as he made to move away, to disappear as silently as he had come. Her smooth brow furrowed as returning consciousness brought pain to her, and then her eyes fluttered open.

They were blue eyes, even more beautiful than he had imagined they would be, large, and clear and reminiscent of the sky on a cloudless summers' day. They stared sightlessly at the ceiling for a moment before shifting to the right to see the man who stood hovering over the side of the high bed, his uncovered face only a few feet above hers.

She blinked once, then blinked again, her eyes widening in disbelief, filling with sudden horror.

And then she screamed. Over and over again, she screamed.

Vincent Nathaniel Mayhew—Earl of Hawkhurst, and once the subject of maidens' dreams, not their nightmares—raised his right hand to cover the left side of his face and fled igno- miniously from the room, Christine Denham's screams following him.

FOUR

"Aunt Nellis, would you be so kind as to stop that interminable pacing? Besides wearing out the carpet, you're quite giving me the headache."

"Christine! You talked to me!" Aunt Nellis whirled about to face the bed. "You know who I am. You're really awake this time, aren't you? Oh, you are, you are! Thank God! Would you like a drink of water? A cup of hot, sweet tea with milk and some toast? Of course you would. You've had nothing but a little broth since the accident."

Christine raised a hand to her pounding head. "Please, Aunt, I beg you, contain yourself, for at the moment I don't consider my condition to be one of overwhelming joy to me. I'm not thirsty, or at least I'm not as thirsty as I am curious. What happened? Where are we? Was there an accident with the coach?"

Aunt Nellis hastened over to the bed, latching onto her niece's hand as if it were the single remaining piece of flotsam in a storm-tossed sea. "You don't remember? Of course there was an accident with the coach. I knew we should never

29

have left that inn after luncheon. Stupid driver! We could all have been killed. You do remember that I told you so, don't you, Christine?"

"And you were so right, Aunt Nellis," Christine admitted, touching her fingertips to the bump on the back of her head and wincing. Under her breath, she added, "Everyone is right at least once, I suppose."

Her aunt went on, not hearing her. "Oh, it was just the most dreadful thing that ever happened. We rolled over and over and I tried to hold onto you but you just bounced about the coach the same way Mavis did that day she stumbled down the whole of the kitchen stairs—you remember that day, don't you?"

"I remember Mavis handing in her notice and going off to work as second barmaid at the Four Crowns," Christine interjected wryly, pushing herself up against the pillows in an effort to make herself more comfortable. "She said, if I recall correctly, that if she were to be tumbled onto her back she'd just as soon be paid for the trip."

"Christine! For shame!" Aunt Nellis exclaimed, her frayed nerves making it impossible for her to remain still for more than one minute. She began pacing the carpet once more, continuing her story. "You've got a nasty bump on the back of your head, which is why you don't remember anything."

Christine smiled wryly. "I'd noticed. But how are you, Aunt? You appear to have come through our ordeal quite unscathed."

Aunt Nellis waved the question away, intent on finishing her tale. "Don't you worry your poor head about me, my dear child. I was unharmed except for a few bruises—although how either of us got out of that coach alive I vow I shall never understand—and the coachman carried you here through the storm. It took forever to get here, and we were so cold. He was really quite brave and strong," she ended reflectively, still rather sad that the man had taken his horses and departed for the village on foot early that morning without even saying good-bye to her. But then, he did have his coach to consider. Someone had to arrange to have it hauled out of that ditch.

"It must have been simply awful for you," Christine commiserated, tentatively stretching her muscles and finding that she was very sore. "But where, please, Aunt, is *here*? This room looks much too pretty to be part of a coaching inn. Are we guests in a private house?"

Aunt Nellis merely nodded, quickly averting her eyes from her niece. "We're on the estate of the Earl of Hawkhurst. We've been here for two days. Two days too long, if you ask me."

"Two days? My, I have been a slugabed. Poor Aunt Nellis, I must have frightened you beyond reason. Two whole days, just imagine. We are unwelcome?"

Aunt Nellis lifted her chin and gave out with a highly unladylike snort. "Unwelcome? It goes beyond unwelcome, my dear. Why, the man positively refused to have us, ordering us back out into the storm to die."

Christine frowned, looking about the large, pleasant chamber once more. "As we are here, and alive, may I then assume that you somehow convinced the earl to have a change of heart?"

Suddenly Aunt Nellis couldn't contain herself any longer. Rushing over to the side of the bed, she took up Christine's hand and poured out all her fears and misgivings, her words tumbling over themselves.

"He wears a black silk cloak and an enormous hood, and he never steps foot outside his study all the day long. He came sneaking in here that first night, while I was taking a short rest from my vigil, but you awoke and screamed, sending him scurrying out like a thief who'd been discovered in the midst of his crime. I believe he's mad, completed deranged. He has a servant, Lazarus, who is so thin and mysterious he positively makes my flesh crawl. Christine—we have to get out of here!"

Christine had lived all of her eighteen years with Nellis Denham and had become accustomed to the woman's love of calamity. She smiled kindly, patting her aunt's hand. "Of course we must, dearest," she said, comfortingly. "He wears a cloak, does he, and a hood? Tell me, Aunt," she could not help adding, "does he limp, or drag one leg, or perhaps have a hideous hump on his back? Do you hear chains rattling as he moves?"

Aunt Nellis threw down her niece's hand in mingled dismay and disgust. "You don't believe me! Christine, how could you be so heartlessly cruel? You saw him. You screamed and screamed —so that I had to hold you down. Don't you remember?"

Christine lifted her hands to rub at her temples. "I remember dreaming, lovely dreams, of being

led to a place where I felt so very safe and happy,"
she said slowly. "But, no, I don't remember a man
being in my dreams. Oh, dear, I hope I didn't
frighten him. He must be very shy. I mean, to be
afraid to show his face!"

"Frighten him? *Shy?*" Aunt Nellis was nearly
overcome. "He is anything but shy. He is
imperious, autocratic, and thoroughly in-
hospitable. Anyone would think he believes we
deliberately planned to land on his doorstep just
in order to inconvenience him. And he's
completely hard-hearted. Imagine, seeking to turn
us back out into the storm. The man is mad, I tell
you. I wouldn't be surprised if we woke up one
morning murdered in our beds!"

Christine, weary and sore as she was, couldn't
help chuckling at her aunt's last contradictory
statement. "I do believe I should like to meet this
terrible host of ours. Surely he joins you for
dinner?"

Aunt Nellis grumbled. "I take my meals in my
own chamber, on his orders. I've never seen him
but the once that first night, and then he hid
beneath his cloak like some criminal. It was all I
could do not to swoon dead away at his feet when
he appeared in the foyer. He was so tall, so dark
. . . so menacing."

"So intriguing," Christine added quietly,
snuggling down under the covers. "Aunt, I fear I
am quite tired. Would it be all right if I slept for a
while as you plan our escape from this place?"

Immediately, Aunt Nellis was all concern. "Of
course, dearest," she assured her niece, tucking
the covers up to Christine's small chin. "I have

been selfish to worry your poor aching head with our troubles. I'll just sit in that chair over there as I have been doing, keeping vigil. Don't worry, Christine. I have your father's pistol tucked beneath the cushion."

"Papa's pistol?" Christine repeated, sleep already claiming her. "Oh, Aunt, you're delicious!"

FIVE

Vincent stood at the ice-etched window, looking out over the terrace to the garden that lay beyond a low stone wall that was now buried under a foot-deep blanket of snow. The garden was a wonderland, each bare branch of the rose bushes clothed in an individual jacket of glistening ice, the evergreens bowing gracefully beneath heavy mantles of blue-white snow.

Yet the heavy flakes still drifted down from a sky white with the stuff, even as the chiming of the mantel clock announced that it was long past the hour of dusk. It had been snowing for three days and nights, and drifts as high as a man's head leaned against the walls of Hawk's Roost and altered the landscape all over the estate.

England was suffering under the longest, hardest winter to hit the island in anyone's memory. Vincent had read in the few newspapers that had gotten through to him that in London the Thames had been frozen from bank to bank between London Bridge and Blackfriars for well over a fortnight in January, making it safe for pedestrians to cross the ice for the first time since the rule of Elizabeth I.

Londoners had made the best of this phenomenon while it had lasted, mounting a Frost Fair on the ice, completed with booths, swings, bookstalls, skittle alleys, toyshops, and even drinking and gambling halls. Vincent had read the accounts with a tinge of sorrow, imagining himself as one of the fair goers, laughing and drinking and gambling, watching his friends as they made rare cakes of themselves chasing the gingerbread girls and trying out skates that had lain idle and rusting since the end of their childhood.

But London was not for him, even if he could have traveled through the frostbound countryside to reach the city. And now, just as the frost had begun to release its crippling grip on the countryside, there had been this snowstorm—this great cold carpet of white that showed no signs of stopping.

He did not mind being locked in at Hawk's Roost. After all, where else would he go? This was his home, his hiding place, his sanctuary, his prison. He would not leave even if he could snap his fingers and have the snow disappear overnight. There was nothing left for him beyond the boundaries of Hawkhurst, not anymore, not ever again.

"Your lordship?"

"Lazarus," Vincent answered, without turning about. "I'm confident you believe you have an excellent reason for disturbing me."

"It's the young miss, your lordship," the servant

informed him, moving about the darkening room to light a single small brace of candles.

Vincent stiffened. "She's no better?"

Lazarus shook his head. "Oh, no, your lordship. She's wide awake, and eating everything Cook can think of to send up to her. Such a nice young lady; very polite and grateful for everything we do for her."

Shutting his eyes, Vincent's agile brain immediately conjured up a picture of Christine Denham as he had seen her that first night, small, vulnerable, and so deathly still as she lay against the sheets. But the picture swirled and changed, so that when it was clear again he saw only her sky-blue eyes opened wide with horror and repulsion as she stared up into his face.

"So, she's awake," he bit out sharply, willing the damning image to leave him. "How very wonderful for Miss Nellis Denham. You must convey to her my congratulations on her devoted nursing of her niece. Perhaps now she will agree to retire to the bedchamber you have prepared for her, taking her great pistol with her, of course. You have removed the ball, I trust?"

"Oh, yes, your lordship! *Um*, your lordship?"

Vincent turned away from the window so that his right profile was visible to the servant. "Now what? Am I to have no peace?"

"The young lady wants a bath, your lordship," Lazarus informed the earl in an awed voice, just as if Christine had asked the servant for the moon and he had no idea of how to fulfill her request.

Vincent smiled, or at least it appeared to be a smile, the servant wasn't quite sure, for Lazarus could see only half of the earl's mouth. Besides, he couldn't recall ever seeing the man smile in the four years he had served him.

"So fearful, Lazarus?" Vincent quizzed. "Has she also requested that you scrub her back?"

"No, sir!" the servant exclaimed, horrified by the suggestion. "It's just that we've been a male household for so long—these past four years with you, sir, and a dozen more before them with your uncle, the late earl, may he rest in peace. We've only the one tub about anymore except for those in the attics, your lordship, and it's in your chambers. I don't know if it will even fit through the door. Please, sir, what do I do?"

Vincent's smile faded and he turned his back to the servant, hiding even his profile from the man. Lazarus's words had immediately brought to mind the vision of Christine Denham's petite body, rosy from the hot, fragrant water, reclining gracefully in the huge tub in front of his fireplace, her heavy mane of curling black hair tied atop her head with a pink ribbon.

She would raise one bare leg to lazily soap it, a huge sea sponge stroking, gliding, from knee to shapely ankle. She would then stand, rising to her feet as a goddess rises from the sea foam, laughing at him as he knelt on the floor beside the tub, tearfully begging her to allow him nothing more than the honor of rinsing the clinging soap bubbles from her glistening body.

The vision splintered into a million pieces as Vincent's fist slammed down on the windowsill. This was impossible. This was insane. He had been alone too long. He had to get Christine Denham out of his house, out of his life, before he turned into a woman-starved beast that would sneak into her chamber at midnight and ravish her.

"Tomorrow morning at ten o'clock. No later, no earlier," he said at last.

"Your lordship?" Lazarus questioned, wondering if he had heard aright.

"My chamber, tomorrow morning at ten o'clock," Vincent repeated evenly, each word costing him more than he dared admit. "Inform Miss Denham that she may have her bath at that time with my compliments."

"Very good, sir. Will you be wanting your brandy now, your lordship?"

"Do I not have brandy every night at just this precise time, Lazarus?" Hawkhurst asked, idly massaging his left shoulder.

"Yes, sir."

"Then I doubt there is any reason why I should deviate from that custom just because Miss Denham has managed to regain consciousness."

But Vincent did deviate from that custom, for later that night, long after the rest of the household—save the loyal Lazarus—was asleep, he called for a second decanter of the mind-dulling liquor.

SIX

Christine had slept so long that now, just past three o'clock in the morning, she found it impossible to get comfortable in her bed. She had stuffed herself on rare roast beef and fresh, home-baked bread—plain fare, but hearty—so that even now her stomach was fuller than she would have liked it to be. She had scrubbed her face and hands at the washstand in the corner, but still she felt dirty and disheveled.

She longed for morning and the bath she had been promised. She'd soak for hours and hours, until her fingers and toes resembled nothing more than soggy prunes, and then she would wash her hair—three times—so that it squeaked as she pulled her fingers through it.

Just the thought of a bath had her hopping down from the high bed to struggle into her dressing gown before pacing up and down the carpet, a movement that was definitely contrary to all her aunt's warnings. Her activity also started up the pain in her head, but she didn't care. Unused to being ill or injured, she was, now that she was conscious, a most uncooperative patient.

According to Nellis, she should be lying quietly in her bed of pain, the covers tucked up beneath her chin, not speaking except to utter an occasional moan or two, and sipping weak broth while listening to bracing sermons her aunt read to her from the prayer book she always carried in her reticule.

But Christine couldn't help herself. She felt young, and healthy, and almost disgustingly fit. Besides, she was unaccustomed to a sedentary life. She wanted to be on the move, doing things—anything.

Walking over to the window, she pulled back the heavy draperies her aunt had closed even as she had begged for them to remain open, to see that the snow had finally stopped and the moon had come out. It was nearly a full moon, so that the garden below her, clothed in what looked like fluffy white cotton and glistening crystal, was nearly as bright as day. She pressed her forehead against the windowpane, the cold from the glass soothing her lingering headache.

So this was Hawk's Roost. It was pretty, very pretty, even as her borrowed bedchamber, full of classic furniture and fine antiques, was pretty. "Not pretty, you country bumpkin," she berated herself aloud. "It's terribly, terribly *modish*. Goodness, Miss Denham, you will never take in Society if you gurgle like a silly miss over anything with just a touch of gilt on it."

A slight frown creased her forehead as she thought of the Season that was to come. Aunt Nellis had been filling her head for years with glowing tales of the goings-on in London in the spring of each new year. It wasn't that she was averse to parties, or gorgeous ball gowns, or handsome gentlemen paying her court. On the contrary, it sounded to be a good deal of fun. Manderley was fairly isolated, and she longed for company more her own age.

It was the financing of the thing that sprinkled her expectations with uncomfortable grains of guilt. Christine's father had left her well taken care of, if she was careful, but her inheritance hadn't stretched to cover the tremendous cost of a London Season, at least not the sort of Season her aunt desired for her.

"I've had a sudden unexpected windfall," Aunt Nellis had told Christine cheerily, but it had been a lie. It had been Aunt Nellis's portion that had paid the rental on the town house in Half Moon Street.

Not only that, but Aunt Nellis's treasured pearl and ruby necklace and her generations-old diamond bracelet that were traveling with them to the metropolis hidden among the woman's undergarments would pay for the many gowns Christine would wear, the ribbons she would buy, the plays and operas she would see, and even the food that would go into her mouth.

Her aunt believed her niece to be unaware of the sacrifices she was making, and Christine hadn't been so cruel as to tell her that she knew the source of their sudden good fortune. But that didn't mean Christine did not think about it.

"I shall just have to marry the first rich man

who wants me," she said into the quiet room, "so that I can pay poor Aunt Nellis back for what she has done for me. What a depressing thought!"

Christine stayed at the window for a long time, lost in a brown study that had little to do with glittering balls and very much to do with a portly old man with gray hair and few teeth bowing over her hand, before a movement below her in the garden caught her attention.

"It's an animal, lost and searching for food," she said, pulling the draperies back a little farther in the hope of improving her view. "No, it's not an animal. No animal is that big. It's a man. A very tall man, all wrapped up in a hooded cloak. It must be Aunt Nellis's monster, the Earl of Hawkhurst!"

Quickly dropping the drapery back into place, she moved about the room, snuffing out all the candles, then tiptoed back to the window and drew the heavy material out of her way. "Now he won't be able to see me seeing him," she said in satisfaction, her breath fogging the windowpane as she eagerly pressed her nose against the glass.

She watched in fascination, holding her breath, as the earl walked across the garden, his long strides made only slightly awkward by the deeply mounded snow. A massive cloak, black as the starlit night sky, molded over his broad shoulders and swirled about his knees as the wind tugged at the material. His legs were quite long beneath the hem of his cloak, his shiny Hessians hugging calves that were neither too thin nor too muscular.

A large hood hid his face from her view, a fact

that bothered her immensely, for she longed to see what her host looked like that he felt the need to hide from his guests. He walked on, moving away from her as the wind gusted, causing him to use his right hand to keep the cloak from opening, exposing him to the cold.

He mounted a small rise about fifty feet away from the walls of the house, standing there for what seemed to Christine to be a long time, his hand now holding the cloak tightly closed at the throat, his face turned directly into the wind, as if challenging the elements in some private game of endurance.

"How excessively odd," she mused, shaking her head, her headache forgotten. "It's as if he's daring the wind to strike him down. Perhaps Aunt Nellis is right. He does seem rather strange. Yet he's standing so straight and tall, like a strong oak. Oh, I wish he'd move closer so that I might see him."

As if in answer to her wish, Hawkhurst turned and began walking back to the house, his right hand once again clasping the front sides of the cloak closed around his middle. When he was just below her window a strong gust of wind whirled through the garden, lifting the loose snow so that it danced around the earl's body like the sea mist just before a storm.

His heavy hood fell back against his shoulders, but the earl didn't seem to mind. He raised his face to the descending moonlight and allowed the swirling snow to caress his cheeks—while unknowingly exposing his profile to Christine's avid gaze.

She inhaled sharply, unable to believe what she was seeing. He had hair as black as hers, as black as night, thick hair that waved only slightly as the wind brushed it back from a forehead that was smooth and clear save for the slashing black brow that sheltered one long, deep-set eye whose color she could not discern.

His nose was perfection itself, straight and narrow, save for a small bump just below the bridge, a forgivable imperfection doubtlessly acquired by an unfortunate collision with someone's hard fist. His mouth was generous, his upper lip nearly as full as the lower, with what looked to be laugh lines vertically scoring the skin below his thin, high cheekbone.

Even his chin was outstandingly perfect, no matter that it was covered with a slight shadow of beard, as if Lord Hawkhurst only allowed himself to be shaved when the spirit struck him.

Christine had seen all this in only a few moments—taken it in as a flower takes in rainwater—letting the reality of it sink into the very root of her, nourishing her body, her soul, before the earl moved directly beneath her and into the house. Her head was reeling with questions, her body reeling with sensations alien to her.

Why was the Earl of Hawkhurst hiding? There was nothing wrong with him, as her aunt had supposed, nothing that would offend or frighten onlookers. On the contrary, he was handsome. He was the most handsome man Christine had ever seen or hoped to see.

She let her forehead press against the window-pane, her eyes closed, her heart still pounding unevenly in her breast. "He's beautiful," she breathed on a sigh.

SEVEN

"**O**h, Aunt Nellis," Christine exclaimed, whirling about, eager to look everywhere at once, "isn't this just the most wonderful room you have ever seen? Look—look over there, at that dresser. It must have a half-hundred golden cherubs carved into its face. This is like a great exhibition. I feel we should have paid a pennypiece each at the door in order to enter. And that tub—it's enormous. No wonder Lazarus didn't want to move it into my chamber."

Aunt Nellis obediently looked around the earl's massive private bedchamber, grudgingly admiring the man's good taste. The entire room was a shrine to classic beauty and expert craftsmanship, she agreed, but somehow the chamber seemed cold to her, and lonely. The softening touches—a woman's touch—were missing. But then, this was a bachelor establishment.

"There are no mirrors, Christine," she said at last, able to voice at least one possible reason for her disconcertment. "Not a single one. Isn't that just the oddest thing? Everyone has mirrors. How else is one to know whether or not one is going about with a piece of meat stuck between one's front teeth, or with one's buttons undone?"

Christine looked up in the midst of admiring an elaborately carved clock that boasted not one, but three faces. "Really? No mirrors? That is a bit odd. Are you quite sure, Aunt?"

Her aunt was standing perfectly still in the center of the room, her face unbecomingly pale. "I've heard it said that the devil can't see himself in mirrors," she murmured, shivering.

Remembering the face she had seen the previous evening in the moonlight, Christine only laughed, running across the room to hug her imaginative aunt. "The devil is it, Aunt Nellis? Now you're sounding as silly and superstitious as Alice."

Aunt Nellis stiffened. Obviously, she disliked being compared to their housemaid at Manderley, a woman who had been known to walk backward through a prickle hedge to avoid coming face to face with Farmer Williamson's gray wagon horse before noon, a woman who wore so many good luck charms and amulets that she rattled when she walked. "I am no such thing!" Nellis protested hotly. "I was merely making a reasonable observation."

"Then observe this," Christine said, pointing toward a door in the corner of the large room. "Obviously we have not seen all of the earl's quarters. I'll wager that door leads to a dressing room, complete with mirrors of every shape and size. Shall I go investigate, both to soothe your jangled nerves and to see if I am right?"

"You shall not," Nellis commanded tersely. "We

all know what happened to Pandora. Besides, I believe I hear the earl's man, Lazarus, coming down the hallway with the first of your bathwater. I wouldn't want him to think you're nothing but a common snoop. My goodness," she continued as the clock struck a single chime, "it's more than time he arrived isn't it? The earl said ten o'clock, and it's nearly half past the hour already."

Christine was instantly diverted. "Dear Lazarus," she said on a sigh. "How sweet he is to have begged the earl for this favor. But he's aptly named, isn't he, the poor soul? I mean, he does look rather moldy, doesn't he, almost as if he has just recently been resurrected."

"Now you're being blasphemous!" Aunt Nellis exclaimed, wringing her hands while giving a silent prayer that heavenly lightning was not about to strike them down where they stood. "I believe that bump on your head has served to sadly rearrange your senses. Drat this terrible weather! Oh, why did it have to begin snowing all over again this morning? Clearly you need the services of a doctor as soon as possible. You may even need to be bled."

"If you think to have some silly old man lay leeches on my body, Aunt, I pray it may snow forever," Christine countered belligerently.

Lazarus entered, carrying two pails of steaming water that he ceremoniously poured into the large enameled tub that stood in front of the fireplace. Four extremely curious male servants, all carrying a brace of buckets across their shoulders, followed him in, and soon the tub was full nearly to the brim. The men lingered once their job was completed, to stand staring at Christine with slackened jaws—at which point Aunt Nellis pointed a finger toward the door and ordered succinctly: "*Out!*"

Christine was already loosening the sash of her dressing gown. "Weren't they cute? You told me this was an entirely male household, but until now I didn't believe you. They acted as if they have never seen a female in her dressing gown before this. You may lock the door after you, Aunt, if it makes you feel better," she said, looking about her for the jar of violet-scented bath salts that Lazarus had delivered to the room earlier.

"But . . . but . . ." her aunt stammered nervously, not wishing to leave her niece alone in this masculine bedroom, no matter how deserted it appeared to be at the moment. "You may need me."

Christine sighed, impatient to be in the warm water. "There are several towels warming before the fire, a pitcher of rinse water for my hair has been placed on an easily reached stool, a clean gown awaits me on that chair over there, and I am fully capable of washing myself—even behind my ears. Please, Aunt, allow me some privacy. I have been bathing alone since I was ten years old."

"You could become faint as an aftermath of your injury and slip beneath the water. Christine, you could drown!" Aunt Nellis ventured, her expression changing rapidly from concerned to horrified. "I'd come back in here and find your hair floating atop the water, your eyes open, staring up at the ceiling!"

Christine looked up at the elaborate stucco

ceiling. "At least I'd have a lovely view," she said teasingly. "Dearest aunt, I don't intend to drown. I promise," Christine added solemnly, all the while liberally sprinkling bath salts in the heated water and then swirling her hand about to raise up mounds of scented bubbles.

But her aunt wasn't finished. Her agile mind had already conjured up another possible calamity. "There could be a secret passageway in here. There often are such things in these old houses, you know. Anyone—even the earl himself —could sneak in here while you're nak—defense-less, and force himself on you."

Christine straightened and began tying up her hair with a pink ribbon. "The earl has not even seen fit to share his dinner table with us. I doubt that he would wish to share my bath. Now, please, Aunt Nellis, go away. The tub will soon grow cold and I shall have to call those dear servants back with fresh hot water."

That consideration was at last enough to roust Nellis Denham from the chamber.

Fifteen minutes later, her clean, wet hair tightly wrapped inside a small towel twisted into a turban, the surface of the bath now covered by a thick layer of bubbles, a clean and thoroughly refreshed Christine carefully leaned her still tender head against the high curved rim of the enamel tub and allowed her limbs to go limp.

This was heaven on earth, she decided dreamily, closing her eyes and allowing the soothing sensation the warm water created to lift her mind away from her troubles so she could float on a higher, happier plane.

The image of the earl as she had seen him in the garden rose unbidden in her head, and she smiled slightly as she remembered how his handsome face showed to such advantage in the moonlight. She had to meet him, speak with him, no matter how shy he was, no matter how he tried to hide from her.

She was not only curious about Hawkhurst, she was intrigued, and more than halfway along in her construction of a fantasy life that would explain him—a life that included a woeful tale of unrequited love and a volume of poems he was doubtless straining to create as he paced his gardens in the moonlight.

Poor man, she sympathized silently, he is obviously obsessed with beauty, if this chamber reflects his interests, yet he hides his own as if ashamed of it. Someone must have once hurt him very, very badly.

"I said you might bathe at ten o'clock. It is now nearly eleven. You abuse my hospitality Do you then intend to stay in there until you melt?"

Christine's eyes snapped open wide in shock and surprise as she sat up, slopping water and bubbles onto the rug, and clutching her oversized sea sponge tightly against her breasts. Her sky-blue gaze hastily scanned the enormous chamber, trying to ferret out the author of this frightening interruption. Somehow, she had gotten herself trapped in her aunt's worst nightmare.

When she didn't answer, the deep, disembodied

voice went on coldly: "Well, girl, are you dumb? Have you no voice? Answer me!"

First he had frightened her, and now he was insulting her. Christine's eyelids narrowed angrily and her winglike brows lifted in challenge as she retorted, "I don't speak with shadows, sirrah. Show yourself."

"I think not," the voice said, although Christine noticed that the menacing tone now had a faint tint of amusement running through it. "You do not appear dressed for visitors."

Christine began feeling the chill of the draft created by an open door somewhere in the chamber. Still trying to locate the source of his voice, which now seemed to be slightly to the left of her, she said, "Yet you, noticing my appearance, were not gentleman enough to retire without bringing my attention to your presence, were you? I believe that makes us even. Now, since I will not speak to shadows and you refuse to show yourself, I suggest that you retire and allow me to quit this tub in peace."

Her head snapped around as the voice, cruelly teasing, suddenly seemed to come from directly behind her. "But how, lovely one, will you know that I have gone, if you can't see my passing? Dare you rise from the safety of your bubbles unless you are absolutely certain you are alone?"

Tears of frustration stung Christine's eyes as she felt like the butterfly her childhood friend James had pinned to a table before slowly ripping off its wings, one by one. He held all the cards, this shadowy earl, yet she had to somehow find a way to strike back at him.

Thinking of James gave her a plan. James had been a tease and a bully, and like all bullies, he had run away when finally she had grown tired of his teasing and dared to call his bluff.

Swallowing down on her fear, Christine faced forward once more and declared forcefully, "I shan't know, shall I, my lord Hawkhurst? Only you will know, only you will see. However, if you are at all a gentleman you will *not* see. You will instead turn your back to me—preferably right now—for at the count of three I am nonetheless going to rise from this tub. One—two—*oh!*"

A light, warm pressure was applied to her bare shoulder and she melted back down into the tub, her heart pounding hurtfully against her rib cage, her vision narrowing as she truly feared she would, for the first time in her life, swoon completely away. Aunt Nellis would indeed return to see her niece's body submerged, her hair floating on top of the water, her eyes staring sightlessly at the ceiling, just as she had said she would.

The thought of coming to so ignominious an end gave her new strength. Slowly turning her head a fraction, Christine saw Hawkhurst's hand, resting just inches above her bare breast.

"Oh," she breathed in a small voice, silently wondering why she hadn't screamed.

The hand was nearly as pale as her own white skin, but it was not soft, for she could feel the scrape of callouses as the hand moved infinitesimally lower, sending her pulse soaring.

It was a large hand, masculine without being

wide, and it ended in long, tapered fingers and well shaped, bluntly cut nails. A plain gold signet ring adorned the second to the last finger of the hand, the hand that burned into her flesh even as it caused a chilling shiver to run through her body.

"Don't, Christine," Hawkhurst said quietly from far above her head, his words nearly lost in the throbbing inside her ears. "Please don't. I'll go now."

The hand lingered a moment longer before lightly stroking the side of her throat and leaving her. She sat completely still, facing front, as a blur of swirling black moved past her tear-bright eyes and left the chamber through a door in the corner.

Only then did Christine begin to cry.

EIGHT

"You're terribly quiet this evening, Christine," Aunt Nellis commented concernedly, laying down her wooden embroidery frame to look over at her niece, who was propped against the bed pillows, her usually sunny expression disturbingly solemn.

"Yes, ma'am," Christine responded absently, staring off into the middle distance.

"I think that bath must have worn you out. I warned you to wait another day, didn't I? Never have I seen anyone with such a penchant for washing themselves from head to toe. Why, when I was your age we didn't find it necessary to submerge our entire bodies more than three or four times a year at the most. Water is not good for anything, not even drinking, some say."

"Yes, Aunt," Christine answered absently, her fingers nervously pleating the bedspread into small, precise folds. "I think water painting is very nice too."

Aunt Nellis rose, smoothing down her gown as she silently congratulated herself. She had been correct. The bath had obviously been too much for the girl. She'd been listless and unresponsive all day, and had barely touched the dinner tray Lazarus had brought up to her.

"It's getting very late, my dear," Aunt Nellis said kindly. "I think it's time you lay down for the night." Crossing over to test Christine's temperature by placing her fingertips assessingly on the girl's brow, she asked, "Are you sure you'll be all right? I could spend another night in here if you'd rather not be alone."

Christine grasped her aunt's hand to lightly rub it against her cheek. "No, dearest, it's time you had some real rest. Lazarus has told me how you have barely slept since the accident. If you don't soon take some time for yourself we shall find our roles reversed, with me nursing you. I'd make you eat gruel, you know!"

Aunt Nellis nodded her approval of this statement. "Gruel is very beneficial to invalids. You're showing some sense at last, Christine. I do believe that is the first really reasonable thing you have said to me since regaining consciousness."

"I'm so glad. I live only to please you, darling Aunt Nellis," Christine teased, pulling her aunt down for a kiss. "Now, go to bed. I'll be fine, really."

Christine waved to her aunt as the woman left the room, but her smile faded once the door closed and she was alone. She had thought this terrible day would never end. How she had ever survived the hours between her strange confrontation with the earl and this moment without her aunt ferreting out exactly what had happened, she would never know.

Yes, she was exhausted. Who wouldn't be? She was exhausted from trying to keep a good face on things while, inside, she was filled with trepidation mingled with avid curiosity.

Christine bit at her thumbnail, a habit she thought she had long since outgrown, trying to find some sense in the earl's actions. He was handsome, yet hid himself. He tried to project total disdain for her and her aunt, yet had been kind to them in so many ways. He purposely frightened her, insulted her, yet he seemed to deliberately call her attention to his existence.

The Earl of Hawkhurst was an enigma, and Christine longed to solve the puzzle that made up the man.

"You should be resting, Christine, not abusing your brains trying to conjure up ways to get to me."

Christine inhaled sharply, sitting up straight in the bed to address the shadow she saw standing in the corner. "You've done it again!" she accused, too angry to feel any real fear. "Can't you ever knock?"

The shadow merely shrugged its shoulders. "It's my house."

"It's my house, it's my house," Christine parroted, making a face. "That may very well be, my lord, but for the moment, this is *my* bedchamber. I did not give you permission to enter."

"Shall I leave?"

"Yes. *No!* Oh, I don't know what you should do!" she exploded, shaking her head. "Aunt Nellis would expire with shock if she knew you were here. But I do very much want to speak with you."

"Permit me to venture a guess as to what you want to discuss. Being a well-brought-up young lady, you wish to thank me for my hospitality, for graciously granting your aunt's demand for shelter."

Christine's eyelids narrowed as she strained to pierce the darkness to get a better look at her visitor. "That goes without saying, my lord, even if I must take exception to your use of the word *gracious*. Aunt Nellis has told me how she had to beg your assistance—although I do thank you for taking us in."

The earl moved slightly, stepping out from behind the chair to lower himself onto the seat, crossing his long legs at the knee. "You give your thanks almost grudgingly, as a child thanks its tutor for having just caned it," he said, his voice so deep, so silky, she could feel the insult slipping over her like a finely spun garment.

Christine leaned forward, now able to just barely make out the shape of the earl's legs as well as the hand that had boldly caressed her throat that morning. More than that she could not see, for his upper body was still shrouded in deep shadow.

"You're playing some private game with me, aren't you?" she asked incisively. "This deliberate baiting serves as some sort of twisted amusement for you. You must be in the midst of experiencing a most dull winter season here at Hawk's Roost."

There was no hint of amusement in the earl's answer. "I did not ask you here, Christine. You seem to have forgotten that. However, if we are playing a game, it is *my* game. And we'll play it by *my* rules."

"How can I do that?" she asked, spreading her hands in defeat. "I don't recognize the game. Is it some form of hide and seek? Then surely I should be allowed to know the location of the secret passageways you use in order to spy on me."

"You don't need secret passageways, Christine," he countered smoothly. "After all, you made very good use of that window over there last night."

Christine sucked in her breath. "You knew I was watching you?"

"I knew," he said, and there was a wealth of sadness in his voice. "But you didn't really see me."

"But you're wrong!" she exclaimed, forgetting to be either tactful or ladylike. "I *did* see you. Your hood blew back in the wind and I saw you. You—you're beautiful! Why do you hide?"

The hand moved, lifting from the arm of the chair to disappear into the darkness. "I'll go now."

"Why?" Christine was in an agony of embarrassment over her candid tongue, but still she persisted. "What did I say that was so terrible? I only spoke the truth."

The earl rose, averting his head, and stepped back into the shadows. "Your truth, Christine. You spoke your truth. Not mine. I overestimated you. You are nothing but a romantic child, with a head filled with nothing more than childish, romantic dreams. Once this storm is over your aunt should take you back where you came from before it is too late. You will be eaten alive in London."

Christine's next words stopped him in his tracks. "A child, am I? Is that why you hid in the shadows to watch me in my bath? Because I am a *child*?"

She watched as he approached the bottom of her bed, his body still in shadow but his hand visible as his fingers lightly traced the intricate lines of one of the sculpted wooden posters. The movement was caressing. Hypnotizing. "You're a beautiful child, Christine. Beauty such as yours *fascinates* me, for it can hide so many ugly, unlovely flaws. What secrets do you hide with your beauty, little one?"

"Secrets?" Christine echoed dully, not understanding. "I have nothing to hide. Whatever would make you think such a silly thing?" She snapped herself to attention, purposefully tearing her gaze away from his stroking fingers to stare down at her own tightly clasped hands. "I can't believe we are having this conversation. You are just an evil man, amusing yourself at my expense. You were right. Please go now. I want you to leave."

Hawkhurst laughed, but it wasn't a pleasant sound. "Never to darken your door again, Christine?"

Where she summoned her courage from Christine would never know, but suddenly she heard herself saying, "Not in this clandestine way, no. Even a romantic child knows not to entertain gentlemen in her bedchamber. But surely we will see you tomorrow evening at dinner, my lord? After all, you are our host."

The hand was withdrawn. The earl's voice was muffled, and Christine knew he had turned his back to her. "I dine alone. It is—easier. But if you wish to flaunt convention and join me in my study once your aunt is abed, we might talk a bit more, or perhaps play a game or two of chess."

"I—I'd like that," Christine answered, fighting the urge to leap from the bed and pursue him into the darkness. "I'd like that very much."

"Now, sleep, Christine. Your aunt is correct. You need your rest."

She merely nodded, knowing she was already alone. Leaning back against the pillows, she debated whether or not she should take up her candle and try to discover the entrance to the passage the earl had used, but in the end she decided to wait for morning before undertaking such a project. She was really very tired, she convinced herself, unwilling to think she was respecting the privacy of a man who, so far, refused to respect hers.

"Now, if only I knew how to play chess," she mused aloud, snuggling beneath the covers.

As the three-sided mantel clock struck the hour of four, Vincent once again used the passageway leading from his quarters to the guest bedchamber in which Christine Denham lay sleeping. He had resisted temptation for as long as he could, but he *was* a man, with a man's weaknesses, a man's desires.

The single bedside candle had long since guttered in its holder, but moonlight streaming through the window Christine had left undraped, as was her custom, cast a many-paneled quilt of illumination across the width of the high-poster bed, lending a soft, almost ethereal glow to Christine's still features.

What was he doing here? Why was he torturing himself this way—and torturing this innocent young girl with his unwanted attentions?

Christine murmured softly, stirring in the bed, then was still once more. He moved closer, knowing he shouldn't. She was so small lying there, her hair so very dark against her pale skin. So very lovely. And so unlike the tall, blonde Arabella.

Arabella. Vincent closed his eyes tightly against the pain the thought of her evoked. She had been so beautiful, so gentle, so unspoiled. So trusting.

And he had killed her just as surely as if it had been his hand that had held the knife that had opened her veins.

Vincent rubbed at the left side of his face, his fingers having long since memorized every inch of skin below his cheekbone. He had been punished for his stupidity, his vanity, his selfish love. Punished first by Fletcher, Arabella's brother and once his best friend, Fletcher Belden—who'd had every right to want to see Vincent suffer—and then, for more than four years, by himself, when Fletcher's revenge had served to do only half the job.

Vincent lived in a prison of his own making, unable to forgive himself, ashamed to go on living while Arabella lay in a cold, unyielding grave. He had borne his penance silently, even gratefully, for a little over four years, feeling he deserved it. But now the pain, at last beginning to ease, had suddenly come back to him twofold.

For now there was this small, dark-haired girl lying in a bed in his house, filling his mind with thoughts he believed he would never have again. Filling him with desire, with longing, with dreams that could never come true.

"Christine," he whispered hoarsely, holding out his hand as he came alongside the bed. "Have I been alone so long that I will dream dreams about any female who happens to stumble unwittingly into my path?"

His hand settled lightly on her hair, its warmth like a living thing beneath his fingers. She slept on peacefully as he gazed his fill of her, tracing the shadows her absurdly long lashes cast on her cheeks, devouring her soft mouth with his eyes.

Could he dare? Would she wake as she had that first time, her liquid blue eyes filled with horror, to scream and scream and scream? By what right did he think to use her this way? But he had to try, he had to know.

His breathing ragged, Vincent slowly lowered his face to hers, the hood he still wore from his earlier stroll in the garden concealing his features. His lips brushed hers lightly, tentatively, then withdrew, only to claim her mouth again, hungry for just one more sweet taste of her.

Christine moaned almost inaudibly, her breath sighing into his mouth, and he hastily backed away, his entire body racked with desire—and something more than desire. Something good, something wondrous, something he knew he did not deserve. She sighed, a slight smile forming on her lips, but she did not open her eyes.

Vincent turned on his heels and fled from the room, back to his own chamber, to fling himself into the chair that sat in front of the fire.

He had been in prison for over four years.

Now he was in hell.

NINE

"Oh, dear, it looks perfectly dreadful out there, doesn't it? So desolate, so eerily bright even at this late hour. Just how deep do you think the snow is now, Lazarus?" Aunt Nellis Denham asked fretfully, peering out one of the floor-to-ceiling drawing room windows, a worried frown on her usually frowning face.

The servant, busying himself with placing the gigantic silver tea tray on the table in front of a settee and then setting out two cups, one for each of the Misses Denham, replied absently, "It's hard to say exactly, ma'am. What with the wind blowing about and all, the snow comes to m'knees in some places and to my rum—" he broke off, then jerked to attention to finish—"er, that is to say, even higher in other places."

Christine lifted a serviette to her mouth to cover her smile. Little did Lazarus know, but the word *knees* was normally more than enough to send her aunt into spasms. The woman must have a lot on her mind not to have already launched herself into a homily on the evils of using familiar terms in female company.

"All in all then, Lazarus," she said helpfully, seeing the man's distress, "you would say there is quite a bit of snow on the ground. Isn't that correct?"

"Yes, miss," the servant answered, shooting her a grateful look as he handed her a cup of hot tea. "His lordship said just tonight as I took his evening meal to him that it looks like the old albatross won't fly any time soon, whatever that means."

"Your reclusive employer has quite a singular way with words," Christine remarked in a choked voice, determinedly spooning sugar into her cup.

The old albatross, not realizing that Hawkhurst had been referring to her or there would have been the devil to pay, turned away from the window to accept the cup from Lazarus's hands. "And now, Christine, tell me," Aunt Nellis said after taking a restorative sip of the hot liquid, "did you enjoy your first dinner downstairs? I rather thought the capon was spiced a fraction too freely, but then I have always had a sensitive palate."

Obviously, Aunt Nellis was trying to impress Hawkhurst's servant with her worldliness. At Manderley, the woman would have been satisfied with a single chicken baked in butter sauce, but Christine was too polite to point that out to her now. Besides, she had other matters weighing on her mind.

Sneaking a quick glance at the mantel clock, Christine only mouthed some random words of agreement and then suggested that her aunt make an early night of it. It was past ten, and she was a mass of nerves about missing her private meeting with Hawkhurst just so that her aunt could practice her wiles on Lazarus.

"Nonsense, Christine," her aunt said dismissingly. "As if a little pepper should send me scurrying to my bed like some missish old woman. No, I think I shall sit up a bit longer, and perhaps work on that embroidery square I brought with me from Manderley. It's the loveliest thing—a scene from the Creation, I believe."

Christine loved her aunt, truly she did, but at the moment she was wishing the dear lady on the other side of the moon.

Narrowing her eyelids, she leaned forward on the settee to peer searchingly into her aunt's face. "How brave you are, Aunt," she marveled, shaking her head. "How staunchly you have stood through these last trying days here at Hawk's Roost, and without a whimper of protest at the heavy physical and mental toll your vigil at my bedside has so obviously wrought."

Aunt Nellis quickly lifted one trembling hand to her face, as if checking for outward signs of damage. "Why do you say that? What do you see, Christine? Am I looking pale? Drat the lack of mirrors in this place! Do I have circles under my eyes?"

Tilting her head to one side, her niece appeared to be concentrating on forming an answer. "No-o-o," she began consideringly, "not actually circles, I don't think. At least, not so much that they cover the puffiness. It was more the rather drawn look that had me concerned."

"I look drawn?" Aunt Nellis's expression took on a look of panic.

Christine sat back against the cushions and waved a hand in dismissal. "But if you say you are feeling fine, then I shouldn't bother about it anymore. I am most probably only imagining things anyway."

Now Aunt Nellis had both hands raised to her face, her fingertips gently probing the skin beneath her eyes. "Puffiness? Really? Perhaps I should consider cucumber slices. And drawn, you said?"

"Just a trifle."

Aunt Nellis traced her rouged cheeks, then tentatively patted at the second chin that was her private woe. "Actually," she said, "I have been feeling just slightly out of coil, not that I wanted to burden you with my troubles, you understand."

"You're too good to me," Christine gushed, willing a tear to her eye. "You cannot imagine how difficult it is for me to stand by silently and watch my dearest companion fade into a dry shell of her former self."

The fingers moved again. "Dry?" Aunt Nellis questioned, pouncing on the damning word. "Why, do you know what, Christine? With all my worries about you, I do believe I have neglected my nightly rituals of late. Yes, you're right, my skin is dry, dry as a leaf in the desert. And I am tired. Bone weary. Perhaps I should make an early evening of it. Perhaps we both should retire to our chambers. Lazarus," she called to the servant's retreating back, "has my small leather bag been brought up to my room?"

The servant quickly assured her that the small leather bag, the one Christine knew to contain at least two dozen assorted creams, lotions, and formulas sworn by their makers to contain magical restoratives guaranteed to return the blush of youth to aging, desperate women, had indeed been delivered to Miss Denham's chamber.

Aunt Nellis rose from her seat, one hand still to her face. "Come along, Christine," she urged, heading for the hallway, "I don't have a moment to waste."

"Yes, Aunt Nellis," Christine answered brightly, skipping a bit as she brought up the rear.

Christine turned her body this way and that, desperately attempting to achieve an angle that would give her a clear view of herself in the small hand mirror. She was wearing her new blue gown, the one the local seamstress had vowed matched her eyes perfectly, but she hadn't yet convinced herself that she quite liked the style. The high waist, as well as the wide, silken ribbon that banded her front to back and hung in streamers behind her, made her feel overly young and rather vulnerable.

"Just what the designer had in mind when creating it, I'm sure," she had told her aunt when first she had seen it. "I believe we are supposed to look endearingly helpless and just slightly vacant in our upper stories in order to be appealing to the gentlemen. No wonder men believe themselves to be our superiors, if we agree to wear dresses that make us appear to be mindless ninnies."

To compensate for this lack of confidence in her

appearance, Christine had earlier crept into
Nellis's chamber to avail herself of a small pot of
rouge. By the light of a single candle she now
smoothed a bit of color onto her lips and then
rubbed some into her cheeks, telling herself that
the action was justified. After all, if the earl could
hide behind the cloak of darkness surely she was
entitled to some armor of her own choosing.

It had been over a half hour since she had at last
been able to bid her aunt good night in the
hallway, and Christine wondered if she could dare
quit her chamber without the woman overhearing
her. Taking a deep breath and then wiping her
suddenly damp palms on a handkerchief, she
decided she could. Her heart was pounding. It was
either go now, she knew, to beard the dragon in his
own den, or she would lose her courage entirely.

A slight scratching at the door nearly had her
jumping out of her satin slippers in fright. "Who—
who is it?" she quavered in a hoarse whisper,
desperately reaching for her dressing gown while
wondering if Aunt Nellis would be able to see the
effects of the rouge in the dimness. Oh, how could
she have been so stupid as to think she, Christine
Denham, who had never gotten away with a single
naughty thing in her life, would succeed now, as
she was about to attempt her most daring
indiscretion?

"It's me, miss. Lazarus," she heard the servant
answer, and she rushed to open the door before
his voice roused her aunt. "His lordship sent me to
say he's waiting on your pleasure." Lazarus had
actually amended his master's words slightly, not
believing it would be helpful to relate

Hawkhurst's message word for word, for the man had said, "Fetch her, man. I grow impatient waiting on her pleasure."

Lazarus did not like the role he had been forced to play. He was a moral man, after all, and this late-night meeting screamed rather than merely smacked of impropriety. But he was also a weak man, who enjoyed his position as well as the luxury of three good meals a day. If Miss Denham was to end up with her skirts tossed over her head it was—as opposed to an abrupt cessation of his own continuing comfort—of no great matter to him.

Christine followed the servant down the hallway, holding tightly to his bony elbow as he held a candelabrum to light the way in the darkened house, tiptoeing down the wide staircase and across the tiled foyer, each step taking her farther from her aunt and closer to adventure. She scrubbed roughly at her face with the back of her free hand, knowing she no longer needed any artificial color to bring a glow to her cheeks.

"Here you go, miss," the servant said at last, opening the door to the study and then drawing back a pace. "His lordship said for me to come back in an hour—no more, no less—to guide you back to your chamber. I'll knock on this door when it's time."

Christine tried to thank the man, but found that no words could push themselves past the sudden constriction of her throat, so she merely smiled and nodded her understanding before stepping inside the earl's study, her body stiffening as she heard the door click closed behind her, effectively locking her inside with a stranger. This was it; there was no turning back now. She had committed herself to whatever was to come.

TEN

It was extremely dark in the room after the brightness of the hallway, a fact that did not surprise her, as she had expected nothing else. The Earl of Hawkhurst seemed to be positively fascinated with the darker hours.

A few candles had been placed about the perimeter of the room and they threw flickering halos of light against the darkly paneled walls, but the main source of light was that created by the fire burning in the hearth. Instinctively, she drew closer to it, and the two wingbacked chairs that faced the fireplace.

"My lord Hawkhurst?" she asked in a thin, choked voice that barely dented the silence.

"My name is Vincent. Vincent Mayhew. I have only been the Earl of Hawkhurst for four years, thanks to a woefully unproductive uncle who carelessly left his title and inheritance to fall to me. The title, quite frankly, is a source of disinterest to me, although I have found his enormous wealth tolerable. I would rather you call me Vincent, Christine."

The earl's voice had come from the depths of

one of the chairs, and Christine prudently lowered herself into its mate, sinking deeply into the soft leather, her legs swinging freely several inches above the floor.

She deliberately averted her gaze from the other chair, staring into the fire so long that her eyes began to sting. "I don't play chess, Vincent," she announced baldly at last, feeling the need to answer truth with truth. "I only wanted to see you again."

"*See* me, Christine?" Vincent echoed, ignoring her confession, which only succeeded in making her feel more guilty. "Am I then reflected in the flames?"

Christine's eyes narrowed as her feelings of guilt disappeared. She lifted her chin, refusing to be baited. "You have made it abundantly clear that you guard your privacy with a vengeance. I am merely being polite, sir. Besides, it is so dark and gloomy in here, I can barely see my own hand in front of my face."

His amused chuckle made her blood boil. "The so proper Miss Denham is reluctant to injure my undoubtedly tender sensibilities, although she cannot hold back her censure. How very kind. How very condescending. And it's killing you, Christine, this not looking at me, isn't it?"

Her hands gripped the arms of the chair until her knuckles showed white, but she did not turn her head. He was so smug. How she longed to do him an injury. "Yes!" she admitted in a tight voice.

"Poor infant. How frustrated you must be, torn between your curiosity and your good manners, doubtless taught to you by your dragon aunt, Miss

Denham, whom you have left dreaming girlish dreams in her chamber while you tiptoe down the stairs to seek delicious danger like some penny-press heroine. But what must be will be, my dear, for this particular Curiosity does not display himself merely to titillate inquisitive young ladies."

Christine had been slowly gaining the upper hand on her temper. Clearly a cool head, not unbridled anger, was needed here. "Really, my lord? And then why, a poor infant can only ask, does this Curiosity skulk in the shadows, if not for purposes of titillation?"

She could hear the resignation in Hawkhurst's sigh, the acceptance of an adversary whose attack he could not deflect with his sarcastic tongue. "You're not a stupid child, are you, to deliberately bait me this way? Almost you force me to frighten you away."

For all her fears, her misgivings, her guilt at having deliberately deceived her aunt, banishment was the last thing Christine wanted. Impulsively, she turned in her chair to look directly at her tormentor. "No! Don't do that. Please don't send me away! *Oh!*"

Vincent's face was once more before her, his physical perfection a profound shock to her entire system. True, his face was partly in shadow, thanks to that confounded hood he seemed determined to wear, but the glow from the fireplace caught and held his features.

Up close, his face was even more intriguing, more compelling. It was a face crafted by a gifted artist with an eye for detail. Every plane, every curve, was cleanly sculpted, his flesh leanly molded around an extraordinary bone structure. His eyebrows were rather low, and slashing, riding the ridge of bone above his eyelids and slightly shadowing his elongated green eyes. They were the eyes of a sensitive man, a caring man, a uniquely appealing man.

His nose was perfectly centered, neither too long nor too short, not overly narrow nor too widely flared, and balanced beautifully above a full mouth that had a vulnerability about it that drew her against her will. Even though his jaw was cleanly square it was not a forbidding jaw, but rather endearingly innocent and, again, vulnerable.

His was the face of a man who had known great joy—and great pain.

Christine looked once more at the silken hood that shadowed most of the left side of his face, seeing the locks of black hair that had tumbled forward onto his forehead. She felt an almost overwhelming urge to take him in her arms, as she would a frightened child, while yet another part of her wildly, wantonly wanted to feel his mouth on hers, to see her face reflected in his sad, gentle eyes.

She reached out a hand to him, almost without knowing what she was doing, what she would do, when something startling happened. Something frightening.

Within the space of a heartbeat the face before her changed. The jaw hardened, the lips thinned, and the light disappeared from his eyes as if they had been candles suddenly snuffed. His expression was now as cold and unyielding as that of a marble statue, remote, and stripped of emotion.

He had looked so young to her. Now he looked at her through the eyes of age.

Christine shook her head, slowly, disbelievingly. "Why?" she asked him, bereft. "Why?"

Vincent didn't have to ask the meaning of her question. He knew that it was much more than idle curiosity that had prompted it. He could see the hurt, the disillusionment, that clouded her innocent eyes.

"I have my reasons," he said tersely. "Only be glad that, even if I have succeeded in burying everything else, I have searched myself to dredge up some forgotten sense of decency, of morality. You had better leave me now, Christine, before I force them back into hiding and take what I want."

"You can't frighten me," Christine said, even as she privately acknowledged that she was frightened down to her toes. Her gaze didn't waver from his face. "I saw your true self before you had time to hide it behind that mask of cold indifference. You would never hurt me. You are much too busy hurting yourself."

"Ah, now the impertinent, audacious child shows herself," Vincent commented, raising his right hand to draw the hood more closely around the left side of his face. "And are you lying again now, as you did when you said you could play chess?"

Christine rejoiced silently, for a hint of softness had crept, unbidden, back into the long green eyes. "I never lied to you. You asked me if I should like to play chess with you. I answered yes, as I would very much like to play chess with you. You never asked if I knew the game."

Vincent rose, his great height making him seem to tower above her seated form. He turned his back to the fireplace, and Christine thought she had at last succeeded in allowing her foolish mouth to lose her any chance of remaining in the room.

But she was wrong. In a moment he was back, placing a heavy chess board on the small table that stood between the two chairs. "If you will look to your right, my dear Miss Impertinence, you will see a small wooden chest I've had Lazarus unearth from some place or another. The chess pieces are inside, awaiting your pleasure. Do you at least know how they are arranged on the board?"

"You—you're willing to teach me?" If it had been somehow possible for Christine to propel herself out of the chair and into a series of dizzying arching, backward flips—like the ones performed by an acrobat she had applauded at the local fair—she would have done it now, for she was that happy.

His smile lit up her world. "I should like to teach you many things, Christine. But we will start with chess. You may be the white queen. I, as it naturally follows, shall take the black."

"Was it ever in any doubt?" she quipped happily, sorting out the pieces, at last feeling free to relax the hold on her tongue without fear of reprisal—or dismissal. "Oh, what a beautiful set this is, Vincent. Just look at these two adorable horses!"

"Knights," Vincent corrected, clearly amused by her untutored appreciation of a hand-carved chess set that had cost him over five hundred pounds. "They are knights, Christine, valiant protectors of your king and queen. I beg you to pay them a little respect."

Christine dutifully saluted the chess pieces, giggled delightedly, lightheartedly, and then smartly placed them where she was bid. "Sir Algernon Balderfield, our closest neighbor at Manderley, is a knight," she added thoughtfully, "and he looks nothing like these horses. As a matter of fact, now that I think on it, Vincent, he rather more resembles a cow—a very old, very fat cow, with a terrible case of the gout."

Vincent's hand covered hers as he helped her place the white queen on the correct spot. "Then Sir Algernon is not to be one of your knights, Christine, for you must have only the best, the bravest, the most loyal about you. Your knights must be willing to die for you—and at least one most probably will, one way or another—before this game between us is completed."

She could barely hear him above the buzzing in her ears. She felt dizzy, just slightly off center, her hand burning beneath his as a tight bud of warmth slowly uncurled in her stomach.

She stared down at his hand, seeing the hand of a sensitive artist, a valiant protector; the gentle hand of a loving father—or the knowing hand of a tender lover. She remembered the way those long fingers had stroked the bedpost in her chamber, tracing the carving almost absently, yet reverently, riveting her attention.

As if under a spell not of her own making, and without a moment's thought as to what she was doing or why she was doing it, Christine slid her hand free, only to clasp his and bring it, palm upward, to cup her left cheek. Slowly, gazing into the shadows that hid all save the question in his eyes, she turned her head and pressed her mouth into his palm.

"Christine."

On his lips her name was a question, a plea, a benediction. A single tear rolled down her cheek to moisten his hand just before he pulled it away, drawing it toward him into the darkness. Slowly, his eyes tortured and raw with pain, he touched his tongue to the tear, taking the salty taste of her into his mouth as her breath caught and held in her throat.

The chess pieces, still for the most part scattered about the board like soldiers belonging to fallen armies, were forgotten as Vincent and Christine spoke to each other without words. Slowly, unable to bear the look in his eyes, Christine allowed her eyes to close, willing him to make the next move, whether it be to advance or retreat.

"You told me to return in one hour, your lordship." Lazarus's voice snapped through the air like a whip, breaking the invisible cord that had bound them together. "It's nearly twelve, sir." As if to prove his point for him, the mantel clock began chiming out the hour, each clear, bell-like sound driving invisible slivers of pain into Christine's heart.

She raised her eyes in time to see Vincent open his mouth, obviously prepared to tear a verbal strip off his diligent servant's hide. His quick anger thrilled her, telling her that he had been as devastated by the last few minutes as she had been.

"Thank you, Lazarus," she said quickly, politely, already rising to her feet before Vincent could speak. "Tomorrow night, my lord Hawkhurst?" she asked, looking down on him, hoping her voice sounded calm.

He was quiet for so long that she began to fear he would refuse to see her again. When he did answer, his response sent her hopes plummeting. "I would consider it an honor if you and your aunt would join me for dinner, Miss Denham."

Clearly, he did not trust himself to be alone with her. The fact that he had invited Aunt Nellis and herself to share his dinner table was only a sop he had offered, probably out of pity. "As you wish it, my lord," she said stiffly, turning away from the sight of the hooded head and the hidden eyes that refused to look into hers.

What a fool she had been, giving in to impulse like a village girl intent on ridding herself of her virtue as soon as possible. She should go down on her knees and thank him for saving her from herself.

She was almost to the door, her chin held high, blinking back tears, when his voice—those deep, velvet tones that were as beautiful as his face—reached across the room to caress her. "And then, later, we shall continue our lessons, Christine, as we did tonight. If *you* wish it."

Christine nearly stumbled, relief making her weak. He had felt it too! This wild, unexplained, unlooked-for attraction. This silent communion. He too was fighting his better self, and losing as handily, and as happily, as she was.

"I wish it, Vincent," she said softly, knowing he heard her, and then allowed Lazarus to usher her back upstairs to her chamber—and her dreams.

How had it happened? How had he *allowed* it to happen, even encouraged it to happen? What had he been thinking of, what maggot of perversity had he gotten into his head that had convinced him he could use Christine Denham for his own personal exorcism, as his own private chess piece, to move about the board as he chose?

She was so young, so innocent, so totally trusting. Like Arabella. No, he corrected, shaking his head. Not like Arabella. Arabella was beautiful, but weak. This girl was strong, for all her slightness, for all her youth. She was strong, and brave, and very, very vulnerable. Christine might bend, but she would not break.

"And she won't give up," he added aloud, staring into the dying fire, oblivious to the chill descending on the room. "Not Christine. She'll continue to invade my life, my dreams, battering at the walls I've built, finding every weakness, every loose brick, until they all come tumbling down around both our heads. Damn it!"

He fairly leapt out of his chair to go over to the window and throw back the drape. The snow lay heavy on the ground, a thick crust of ice holding it in place even where it had drifted against the window frame. It would be a week or more before he could safely send Christine from his house, longer if it snowed again.

How would he ever keep his hands off her for that interminable amount of time? How could he ever let her go when that time was over?

His hands. Vincent looked down at his left hand, hanging uselessly at his side, and shook his head. He was overreacting, his solitary life having dulled his wits. He'd had two hands to hold Arabella and she had slipped away from him. Did he really think he could hope to hold Christine to him—or away from him—with only one?

A real, physical ache invaded his chest as he realized that he might never know what it was like to hold Christine to him with both hands. Yes, he had been experiencing quite a lot of pain these last six months, pain the doctor had once told him to pray for, as it would signal that some of the injured nerves and muscles had at last decided to come back to life, weaving their way along twisted paths to reform connections that had been so savagely ripped apart.

But some pain, some disturbing tingling, was not enough. There was no strength, no ability to take life into his hand and crush it, or cradle it. Returning to his chair, he reached over and picked up the white queen, turning the figure this way and that, looking for the flaw. There was always a flaw, if you looked closely enough. At last he saw it, a faint discoloration in the wood just at the base, barely noticeable, but there just the same.

He lifted his hand, about to fling the imperfect figure into the dying fire, but then his arm stilled, for this chess piece represented Christine, his white queen, his possible salvation.

Lifting his left hand into his lap, he laid the piece across his palm, pressing the wood into his skin until he could feel its sharp edges summoning the pain it was so important he feel.

Slowly, reverently, he used his right hand to curl his numb fingers gently around his queen.

ELEVEN

*T*he winter-bright sunlight, reflecting off the endless expanse of ice-coated snow, was so brilliant it stung Christine's eyes. She couldn't remember ever seeing so much snow, or ever being happier to see it. The elements had trapped her inside the confines of Hawk's Roost, surrounded by a world turned white, and there was no place on the entire earth she'd rather be, because Vincent Mayhew was locked up here as well.

She looked up at the sky, hoping to see banks of gray clouds rolling in from the west with the promise of even more of the fluffy confection, but the sky was depressingly clear. Refusing to be downcast, she wrinkled her nose, dismissing the need for another storm for, after all, the snow of the high drifts was already tumbling into her boots.

"Besides, it's so cold none of it will begin to melt for days and days," she assured herself as she struggled to make her way through a particularly high drift. "And then, once the thaw does come, the roads will be far too muddy for a carriage.

89

Why, it could be four or five weeks before Aunt
Nellis and I can remove ourselves to London."

Lazarus was standing up against the wall of
Hawk's Roost, trying to hide his thin body from
the wind, his arms wrapped tightly about himself,
three long woolen mufflers in danger of cutting
off his supply of frigid air. He pulled down the
mufflers reluctantly when he heard Christine
speak. "You said something, miss?"

Christine looked behind her, immediately
feeling sorry for the servant who was outside only
because of her. Aunt Nellis, once she had been
badgered into allowing her niece a short excursion
into the garden, had adamantly demanded that
Christine have an escort.

"You never know what sort of terrible hooligans
could be hiding outside in the bushes, just waiting
for an innocent young girl like you to happen
along," her aunt had declared earlier, causing
Christine to wonder, not for the first time, just
how active—and possibly lurid—Aunt Nellis's
imagination might be.

"It was nothing, Lazarus. I was just talking to
myself," Christine assured him quickly, politely
trying not to notice that the poor man's nose was
running. "Please, Lazarus, go back inside. My aunt
has doubtless gone to her chamber for a nap, so
she will never be the wiser. I shall be just fine, I
promise."

Lazarus fought a quick battle with his
conscience, which just as quickly lost the war
against the demands of his very cold, very wet
feet. "If you really think so, miss," he agreed,

already racing for the nearest door as fast as his thin legs and the deep snow would allow. "Don't you be too long now, miss, please, if you will. Ten minutes more or less, or else you'll catch your death and your aunt will be terribly displeased with me."

Christine called her agreement, then waved the servant on his way, happy to be alone. Her Aunt Nellis may have denied her horses, or the freedom of the village, but she had always encouraged her niece to enjoy the pleasures of the outdoors, so that Christine had grown up hating the feeling of being enclosed day in and day out by four walls.

Of course, Nellis Denham's idea of the out of doors did not include stumbling about knee-deep in snow in the dead of winter, but Christine didn't mind the cold weather. It was exhilarating, feeling the sharp bite of the wind against her cheeks, and listening to the silence of a countryside muffled in snow.

Christine bent down beside a winter-barren rose bush to admire the way last night's short rainfall had sheathed it all over in a thin layer of ice. Slipping her hand out of her fur muff, she ran her fingertips up and down the length of one slim branch, tracing an ice-dulled thorn with the tip of her index finger.

"You enjoy flirting with danger, don't you?"

Christine, startled into sudden movement, felt the thorn prick her skin and quickly brought her fingertip to her lips, sucking a small drop of blood into her mouth as she looked at him balefully.

"You are nothing if not consistent, Vincent," she

said after a moment, trying not to let him know how happy she was to see him. "You must enjoy sneaking up on people, even out here."

This afternoon Vincent was clad in a heavy black woolen cloak that was molded to his broad shoulders and descended in deep folds to end at the tops of his shiny Hessians, a muffler covering the lower third of his face. He looked dark, and mysterious, and Christine was, as always, thoroughly entranced.

He swept her an elegant leg—or at least it might have been elegant if he had executed it in a drawing room. Here, in the snow, it was almost comical, and Christine's light, musical peal of laughter mingled with the breeze that danced past his bowed head.

"I passed by poor Lazarus, illicitly toasting his skinny feet at my fire in the study, and he told me you had escaped the house for some fresh air," he said, as if he needed to explain his presence, stepping forward to walk at her left side as they made their way down what, in warmer weather, would be one of the bricked garden paths. "He was mumbling something about hooligans, I believe, so I thought it best to lend you my protection."

"And who, I must ask, is to protect me from you, my lord?" she dared to venture, peering impishly up at him from under the brim of her hat. "That scarf makes you look much the hooligan yourself."

Christine had spent most of the past night reliving their time together in his study. She had succeeded in banishing any lingering fear of this strange man, as well as her embarrassment over her own actions. All that was left was her over-whelming need to be near him, to hear him, to see him.

Vincent looked down at her and she could see faint creases appear around his eyes, surely a hint that he was smiling at her. "I believe I should be asking that same question of you, Christine," he countered easily, his deep voice made even more appealing by the soft barrier of wool that kept part of his expression hidden from her. "I have never felt so much danger in my life as I do when I find myself in your presence."

"Thank you, Vincent," Christine replied cheekily, slipping a hand around his arm as they climbed the slope that led to what she assumed was a small rise overlooking the east end of the grounds. It had been just at the crest of this small knoll that she had first seen him standing alone, facing down the elements. "I don't believe I have ever been called dangerous before. I think I rather like it." She looked about as they walked on and said, "Oh, it's so beautiful here, isn't it? So peaceful and serene."

His look was considering. "Yes, you would think that, wouldn't you?" he said softly, slipping his arm free so that he could take her hand in his. "Come with me, dangerous lady, and I'll show you real danger." Tugging on her hand, he led her to the top of the gentle slope, stopping just as they reached the edge of a sheer cliff that fell away fifty feet or more to the flatter land below.

It had been so sudden. One moment they had been safe, secure, strolling through a winter wonderland, and the next moment they were poised on the edge of a precipice, in imminent danger of falling to their deaths.

Christine's smile faded and she turned to him, holding onto his arm with both hands as she buried her face against his shoulder. "That's not funny!" she declared, hating the way her voice shook. He had looked so serene that night in the garden, yet he had been deliberately flirting with death, even courting it! Why? "I didn't know this cliff was here."

"There are times life doesn't afford us the luxury, or the curse, of knowing what lies ahead." Vincent stood very still, feeling her tremble against him, hating himself for his impulsive action.

He knew how she felt. He hadn't known his own particular cliff had been there either, waiting for him to stumble, not until he had been tumbling down it, turning over and over until his life lay smashed and broken at the bottom. His life, and Arabella's life, and Fletcher's life.

"I'm sorry, Christine," he said, meaning it. "I think I was trying to teach you something in my own obscure, twisted way. Come along now, we should return to the house before we are missed."

"No, not yet, please. I want to stay here a minute longer, and look." Something inside Christine told her that this was an important moment, important for Vincent as well as herself.

She stood firm, willing herself to peer downward, past the edge of the cliff and at the land below. "I don't think I was as much frightened as I was surprised, Vincent. And yes, I know that we are not privileged to know our fates in time to avoid some heartache. But we wouldn't really be living our lives to the full if we knew everything, would we? We'd merely be acting out a part where we knew all the lines, could anticipate all the moves. I should think that would be very boring."

"Yet infinitely safer," Vincent added, slowly drawing her back, away from the edge. She was making him decidedly nervous. "You are very young, Christine. An infant. You really haven't lived yet, you haven't had time. Life is perfect for you, perfect and beautiful. But nothing is so beautiful that it cannot be destroyed, snatched away when you least suspect it. When you get to London and are surrounded by handsome young men begging for your hand, you will remember that, won't you?"

Christine was still holding tightly to his arm. "London," she muttered, her head down as she minded her steps. "I had almost forgotten my debut. It's Aunt Nellis's idea, you know. She has such high hopes for my future. I think she is living her life over again through me, poor dear. She never married, you know."

"Yes, I had gathered that," Vincent said, so that Christine couldn't be sure just what he had understood about her aunt, although she was fairly certain he could see through the older woman as if she were a freshly scrubbed pane of glass.

"We really can't afford a Season," Christine blurted out, feeling she could tell him anything and he would understand. "As it is, Aunt Nellis had to wait until now, when I am about to turn eighteen, to have her dream for me come true. She means to sell her jewelry."

"The pearl necklace and the diamond bracelet, I imagine," Vincent said, nodding his head.

Stopping in her tracks so that he had to halt as well, Christine exclaimed, suddenly feeling violated, "Well, is there anything you don't know? Tell me, how many gowns are packed in my trunks? How many gloves? How many ribbons for my hair? How dare you!"

Vincent turned to take her hand, dragging her along behind him. "You are overreacting, Christine," he warned coldly. "I live a solitary life here, and discourage visitors. Having two unchaperoned ladies tumbling onto my doorstep was unexpected, to say the least. I had Lazarus check your luggage that first night as a matter of course, just to confirm your aunt's story."

Christine sniffed derisively, nearly stumbling as she tried her best to keep up with the furious pace he was setting. "I don't believe you. What possible danger could two ladies pose the great Earl of Hawkhurst? And I was unconscious, for heaven's sake! Really, Vincent, I know I am young, but I'm not entirely stupid. And stop running—I'm not a giant either, like you!"

Vincent stopped abruptly, behind a tall evergreen that blocked any view of them from the house, so that Christine roughly cannoned into his chest.

He did not apologize, but only stepped back a

pace, putting a small space between them. "I have been, in past years, the object of some curiosity, Christine, although the tongues should have stopped wagging by now. I admit it. I overreacted. You hadn't misrepresented yourselves to gain entry to my home."

"Thank you for that kind admission," Christine said nastily, still slightly breathless and not convinced she shouldn't be angry.

"But that does not mean your presence here isn't the greatest danger to my solitude, my hard-won peace, that I have ever faced," he went on, his voice hard. "God, Christine, don't you know yet? Haven't you guessed why I hide myself away here like some wounded animal? The other night, when I told you my name, I thought you might have made the connection, but you didn't. You must be the only person in the whole of the British Empire not to have heard the story."

Christine's heart was beating so fast, so hard, it hurt. She was too close to him, her face upturned so that she could see the naked pain in his eyes, feel the warmth of his breath as it formed vapor clouds in the cold air. "Manderley . . . Manderley is very isolated," she explained nervously, longing to wrap her arms around him, to lend him her comfort. "Scandals grow very cold before they reach us."

"Scandal?" Vincent's tone was scathing. "What unlovely names the world puts on heartbreak. How the world sniggers behind its hands at despair, at the needless waste, the horror of it all."

"Tell me, Vincent," Christine begged, placing

her hands on his chest, her muff tumbling to the ground, forgotten. "Nothing is so bad that it cannot be shared."

"Nothing, Christine?" he repeated bitterly, staring at some empty space a few inches above her head. "This scandal, as you call it, was considerably more than a nine days' wonder." He looked down at her for a long moment, then raised his hand to lightly cradle the back of her neck beneath her collar. "Do you know what the worst sin of all is, infant? The very worst sin man can commit, his worst, most damning failing? It's love, Christine. Not theft, not murder, not even treason. Love."

Christine was frightened, more frightened than she had ever been in her young life. Vincent was on the brink of telling her something, something that would force her to change her opinion of him, something that might destroy their tenuous peace. "Stop this! You're speaking nonsense. I don't want to hear any more! We were strolling in the snow, nothing more. Please let me enjoy your company," she begged fiercely, pressing her face against his chest.

He stood his ground, not touching her. "This was never a simple stroll, Christine. From the first, our times together have never been simple. Last night taught me that you have the right to know who, and what, you are dealing with when you dare to be with me."

"No! Whatever happened to you, whatever great sin you think you are guilty of, you are different now than you were before—I'm sure of it. You have to stop hiding yourself away like some terrible criminal. Surely you have been punished enough?"

Vincent's large hand cupped the side of her face, his fingers laced through her hair. "I had begun to think so, Christine, until you landed on my doorstep. Now I believe my punishment has only just begun."

She wanted his arms around her, but he continued to hold her loosely, denying her his strength. Slowly, as they stood in silence, she gathered her own courage and voiced her private conclusions as to why he hid his face from her, from the world. "You have been injured in some way, haven't you, Vincent? The left side of your face, I imagine, as you are always so careful to keep it averted from me. Were you in a duel?"

She could feel him taking a deep breath, then releasing it in a shuddering sigh. His voice, when he spoke, was deadly cold and emotionless. "I killed a woman, Christine. I loved her, and my love killed her, and her brother quite rightly took a horsewhip to me. When he was done my left arm was nearly severed and my face—my face was cut."

She lifted her face away form his chest to look up into his eyes. He was staring straight through her, as if she had already turned away from him. She could feel her head begin to slowly move back and forth, silently contradicting what she had heard.

His physical scars, no matter how terrible they might prove to be, were secondary now. What was left of his physical beauty was more than enough for a half dozen men. It was the injury to his soul that was causing her this almost unbearable pain. She had to prove that his scars didn't matter to her. "I don't believe it. It must have been an accident. The brother was wrong. You could never hurt anyone, especially someone you loved. Please, Vincent, don't hide from me anymore."

She knew what she had to do. When he didn't move away from her, didn't refuse her request, Christine slid both hands slowly up his chest to touch the muffler that he had employed to hide himself from her. He still didn't resist, but only continued to stare through her, his eyes devoid of emotion, as if preparing himself to deal with the disgust his face would cause.

Swallowing hard, her fingers trembling, fearful of what she would see, she pulled the soft wool away, baring his face to her in the brilliant sunlight.

There were three scars. Three long, thin, white lines that mocked the perfection of his face and throat. One seemed to trace the line of his jaw almost lovingly, to fade just below the center of his chin. The second scar stretched from the center of his cheekbone to the corner of his mouth, while the third began just beneath his ear, to disappear into the collar of his shirt.

Once, they must have been terrible. Once, they would have been deep, and red, and very, very painful. Now they were faded, almost attractive, as they lent a rakish maturity to his youthful good looks.

Yet, as she stole a quick look into Vincent's eyes, she knew that he didn't, couldn't, see his scars that way. To him they were still as they had been, raw, and ugly—and a constant outward reminder of the heartbreak that had caused them to be carved there in the first place.

She wanted to weep for him, but she knew he wouldn't understand. He would think she pitied him.

She wanted to rail at him for his terrible self-inflicted punishment that far outstripped any revenge that had been wrought by the grieving brother, but she couldn't. This was no time for a sermon.

Slowly, fearful that he might run from her, she lifted a hand to stroke his cheek, desperate to heal the inward scars that were a hundred times more damaging than these thin white lines.

Standing on tiptoe, her body pressed tightly against his, returning stare for stare, she tilted her head slightly to one side and touched her lips to his, showing him without words that, to her, he was still the perfect Vincent of the moonlight, and still welcome in her life. As the heat of his mouth melted her fears, she sighed, slowly allowing her eyes to flutter closed.

Vincent's strong right hand, raised in the act of pushing her away, stilled, and formed itself into a tight, trembling fist. He couldn't do it. He couldn't make himself do the right thing—the honorable thing.

He needed her too much.

Slowly his fingers opened, and he lowered his hand to clasp her waist as he allowed himself to be pulled more firmly into her embrace. His mouth crushed hers, hungry, searching, seeking, tasting the forbidden fruit. She was so soft, so open, so giving.

It was all so wrong.

It was all so right.

"Christine," he breathed hoarsely when at last the kiss was over and her head was once more pressed against his chest. "Christine."

"*Christine!*"

He felt her stiffen, then move away from him. "It's Aunt Nellis," she said unnecessarily as he quickly slipped the woolen muffler back over his face. "I must go. I—I don't want to go, to leave you like this. Oh, Vincent . . ." There was so much she needed to say, so much he needed to hear.

"*Christine, where are you?*"

She kissed her fingertips, then pressed them to his cheek. "Tonight?"

Vincent nodded, clearly not trusting his voice, then stayed behind the tree, out of sight, as she walked back toward the house, calling out, "I'm here, Aunt Nellis. Go back inside before you take a chill."

"Tonight," Vincent repeated softly, dropping to his knees in the snow to lift Christine's muff and rub it against his cheek. "Dear God, I have to put an end to this before it's too late—for both of us!"

TWELVE

Vincent took his dinner alone while Christine and her aunt had their meal in the formal dining room, thankfully situated at the opposite end of the house. He had broken his promise to join them there, choosing to hide himself in his study, away from Christine's searching eyes, safe from her sure-to-be-probing questions.

"She's a child. A foolish, romantic child. She has no real experience of love. She doesn't know what she's doing, what she's daring," he told the uneaten food congealing on his plate. "She sees me as a challenge. The poor, tragic reclusive earl, hiding a scandalous secret, bearing scandalous scars. I should demand that her aunt confine her to her chamber until the roads are passable."

He reached over to ring the bell that sat on the table beside him. "Lazarus," he ordered when the servant appeared almost immediately, as if he lived his life just outside the study door, waiting for his master to summon him, "kindly convey my regrets to the ladies and tell them that I am indisposed for this *entire* evening."

"*All* evening, your lordship?" Lazaraus asked,

clearly referring to Miss Denham's proposed visit once her aunt was abed.

"All evening, Lazarus," the earl pronounced flatly, motioning for the servant to remove the dinner tray. "Surely my request wasn't that convoluted. I wish to be alone. Just leave the decanter on the table on your way out. I don't care to be disturbed again."

"Very well, sir, if you think it's for the best," Lazarus said, obviously approving.

"It is such a comfort to me, dear Lazarus, to know that I have pleased you," Vincent said softly as the servant exited. He stood, shaking his head free of the hood he had forgotten he was wearing, then allowed the cloak to shrug off his shoulders onto the floor, to lie there, a swirl of black silk blotted against the pale carpet.

He walked to the cabinet that doubled as a writing desk and unlocked a drawer, pulling out a gilt-framed miniature, then returned to stand before the fire.

The painting he held was that of a woman, a very young, very beautiful woman. Her smile was warm, her blonde head tipped forward demurely, her soft brown eyes gazing lovingly at something or someone just outside the picture. The likeness was so very lifelike, he half expected her to turn and speak to him.

Arabella. How he had loved her. He had loved her to death.

He studied the portrait for a long time. He tilted it this way and that in the firelight, searching, as he had searched for over four long years, looking for the flaw until he found it, just as the artist had found it—just there, in her averted gaze.

Arabella had been more than demure, more than docile. She had been weak, too fragile to look life in the eye. Why had he never noticed her instability, her emotional turmoil, when there had still been time to save her?

Over the past four years Vincent had become obsessed with the search for hidden flaws in what seemed to be perfection, looking for proof of his theory that life was a liar, that nothing was perfect, no matter how perfect it should appear. Nothing was flawless, happiness was never permanent, no emotion was to be trusted.

Vincent's own flaw, as he saw it, had been even deeper below the surface—hidden even from himself—carefully tucked behind the "pretty face" Fletcher had so successfully stripped to the bone. His flaw had been that he had loved too much—his blind, selfish, destructive, all-consuming passion to possess Arabella, body and soul.

Perhaps that was why he had accepted his penance so willingly, almost gratefully. He had known that he was guilty. He, and not poor, destroyed Arabella, lying in her grave for over four years. The real crime hadn't been hers. It had been his. It was still his. It would always be his. Even now, when Christine had become his reality, and his love for Arabella was only a dim, painful memory.

But his scars, his useless arm, these were more than memories. They were the permanent, outward reminder of his guilt, and it was those reminders that kept him hidden away here at Hawk's Roost, where he could do no more harm.

"I'll make sure you never destroy another innocent young girl with that pretty face of yours," Fletcher Belden had shouted as he wielded his whip, his words cutting into Vincent more painfully, more tellingly, than the leather thong.

But Fletcher Belden couldn't have known that a woman like Christine existed, a woman who would stumble, unwanted, into Vincent's life and dare to look past the scars to see the man.

Vincent lifted his face to the ceiling, his breathing tortured. "Once more, I love too much, want too much. Oh, Christine, Christine. God help me, how will I ever find the strength to let you go?"

THIRTEEN

The door to the hallway had been carefully locked from the inside.

Every candle save one in the room was lined up atop the small side tables that had been carefully pushed near the far wall in order to help illuminate the carved wooden paneling.

The remaining candle was in Christine's hand, and she moved it slowly up and down in front of the paneling, searching for any slight distortion in the wood that would show her the location of the hidden door.

"It has to be here," she told herself as she held the candle high in its holder, watching to see if the flame would dance in a slight draft coming from the secret passageway Hawkhurst had used to enter her room.

The yellow flame flickered, but only because her breath had stirred it. "Blast it all! It has to be here somewhere. It just has to!"

Setting the candle on one of the tables with a frustrated thump, she raised both hands to the paneling, sticking her fingertips into the wooden rosettes that decorated it, probing for some hidden release mechanism. Nothing happened.

Christine was beginning to feel a little desperate. She dropped to her knees, pulling back the edge of the carpet to press her hands against the bare floorboards. She sneezed twice as she raised dust the male servants of Hawk's Roost had neglected for decades, but nothing more productive happened.

She released her breath in an audible whoosh. "Hang you for a horse thief, Vincent Mayhew, I give up!" She reached for the edge of a small bookcase set into the corner, planning to use it for leverage as she stood. Her hand grasped it just at the left corner, her thumb pressing against the fleur-de-lis pattern.

"*Oh!*"

Magically, a ceiling-high, three-foot-wide section of paneling disappeared, neatly, soundlessly, sliding behind the adjoining section. A cool, only slightly dank draft slipped into the room, so that her shiver could be more easily put down to excitement rather than the cold.

Hurriedly scrambling to her feet, Christine brushed down the skirt of her pink muslin gown and picked up her single candle. She took a deep breath, counting to ten, trying to steady her resolve.

This was the moment of truth. She had spent three hours preparing herself for dinner earlier that evening, only to have to face her aunt's probing questions as to why her niece would wear one of her best gowns for a simple country meal, all the while being silently mocked by a vacant chair at the head of the dining table.

She had waited impatiently, but in vain, for Lazarus to come scratching at her door—ready to escort her once more to Hawkhurst's study —anxious to hear his explanation for having lied to her, her abused emotions running the gamut from confusion, to despair, to downright anger.

It was this last emotion that had finally succeeded in gaining the upper hand and just before midnight had at last sent her scurrying about her chamber, gathering candles to help her in her search for the secret panel. Now, more than an hour later, she had found it.

"The question remains," she told herself rue-fully, still staring at the empty black hole, "just what are you going to do about it?"

She felt that she had right on her side for, after all, he had promised to dine with her. He had promised he would see her in his study. He wasn't ill, Lazarus had assured her of that. And he certainly hadn't left the estate—in this weather he would have to be gifted with the secret of flight in order to get past the walls.

No, she was convinced he was hiding. Hiding from her. Hiding from what he termed the ultimate sin—love. "And," she declared, defiantly raising her small chin, "he is simply *not* going to get away with it!" Her decision made, Christine carefully lifted her skirts and daintily stepped over the low threshold, and into adventure.

Adventure took her no more than three steps before it hit her square in the face in the form of a

sticky spider web, and she had to cover her mouth
to hold back a maidenly screech as she fought to
free herself before the spider made a nest in her
hair.

But she persevered, for she was made of stern
stuff. Holding the candle in front of her, she kept
on walking, noting that the passageway was not so
well used that the earl's footprints did not show in
the dusty, uneven floor.

The passageway was not exactly what she had
expected. There might have been steps, she had
thought, leading down to the earl's study, or this
particular passageway could have led her into a
greater network of secret passages and tunnels
that honeycombed the entire structure. But it was
just a single corridor, with only one other logical
outlet—Vincent's bedchamber.

A prudent female would have turned back at
this point, barring the door behind her, but
Christine couldn't do that. If she was about to do
wrong, she was going to do wrong for the right
reasons.

Idly, just to keep her mind occupied, she
wondered to what purpose other earls of
Hawkhurst had put this secret corridor. Had one
of his lordships used it to visit his mistress? "He
certainly wouldn't have needed it to visit his wife,
you idiot," she informed herself ruefully.

Her head down, she followed Vincent's
footprints for what seemed like miles, but which
in actuality was less than fifty feet, before coming
up against another seemingly impenetrable
wooden wall. "Here we go again," she groused,
sighing.

She looked at her candle, distressed to realize that it had burned quite low and was in danger of sputtering out before she could even make it back to the safety of her own chamber.

She turned around, thankful to see that the multitude of candles still burning in her chamber cast a faint yellow glow in the distance, but the sudden presence of an indignant, scolding mouse ten feet behind her had her once more concentrating all her efforts on going forward.

Scanning the wall frantically, she saw a round iron pull ring just above eye level. Obviously the need for secrecy was not as important once inside the passageway. She closed her eyes and gave the ring a strong tug. The solid wall slid silently away.

The mouse chattered at her again and Christine hurried to step through the narrow opening, to find herself in the chamber she had been in once before, to bathe—Vincent's bedchamber.

"Where did you think you'd end up, you silly creature, in the dairy?" she berated herself out loud, knowing that she had just passed beyond the pale. She had deliberately set out to beard the lion, as it were, in his den. Now she was here, and it was too late to turn back.

Very definitely too late.

His voice made her jump, coming to her as it did out of the darkness.

"It would appear my bad habits have served to set you a poor example, Miss Denham. Or am I wrong, and you have accidentally stumbled into my room on your way to visit your aunt? Never fear. I forgive you. It was a most logical mistake. The well-lit hallway—a dark, musty passage. I can quite readily see how you must have gotten the two of them confused. As a matter of fact, I won't even mention that I have been sitting here for over an hour, listening to you tap, tap, tap against your chamber walls."

"Oh, be quiet, Vincent," Christine commanded pettishly, trying very hard to get her suddenly racing pulses back under control.

He was here, in the darkened chamber, but she couldn't see him. Her sputtering candle was no help to her, so she blew it out, tempted to hurl the pewter holder against the nearest wall. Useless thing! She was in the dark, with no idea where he was, with not a single idea what she would say to him if she could see him, and no way to make any but an ignominious exit if she decided to make a run for it.

Obviously, she had been wise not to run off to the continent to offer her services to Wellington as a spy. She wouldn't have lasted a moment behind enemy lines.

"Where the devil are you, Vincent? I can't see a thing past the tip of my nose."

"And a lovely nose it is," he answered, seemingly amused by her predicament, "if a bit long. All the better to poke into my business, I imagine."

"Keep talking, if you please," Christine begged sweetly, advancing into the room, trying to locate his position by the sound of his voice. "I'd like to find you so that I might return your insults."

He laughed aloud at her impertinence. She moved toward a chair in the far corner, somehow knowing that he was there, far from the light cast by the fire, hiding.

"I'm not moving, Miss Denham. I have nowhere to go, it seems, where you will not hunt me down. Tell me, has anyone ever used the word pernicious when referring to you, little brat?"

"You consider me to be wicked, Vincent?" Christine couldn't keep the pain out of her voice.

"I consider you to be a somewhat *fatal* young lady," he answered simply. "Ah, here you are at last. Congratulations on the successful conclusion of your little expedition. Good evening, Christine."

Christine stopped in front of the wingback chair, the fireplace at her back. She leaned forward slightly, trying to make out his form in the darkened room. "Good evening yourself, my lord Hawkhurst. Why didn't we see you at dinner?"

He sighed, fatalistically, as if he had been expecting the question. "Why did I reject you? That is your real question, isn't it, Christine?" he inquired softly, almost kindly. "Your entire posture speaks most eloquently of injured pride."

"As your retreat from me speaks most eloquently of your fear of life, Vincent," she returned, once more letting emotion make a shambles of her best intentions, yet not caring that she might be making a fool of herself. "Oh, Vincent," she cried, falling to her knees in front of him, her hands closing convulsively on his thighs, "why? Today, in the garden, we were so close. It was so wonderful, so very special. I thought we had reached an understanding. Why are you doing this to me—to us?"

His right hand, folded over his left in his lap, tentatively reached out to her, then just as quickly withdrew. "Do get up, Miss Denham," he ordered coldly. "You are making a fool of yourself."

Christine looked down at her own hands, realized where they were, and immediately removed them, to sink back on her heels. "Then you—you don't care for me?" Her voice was small, and injured.

Vincent's next words tore into her, assaulting her with the force of physical blows. Even in the darkness she knew that he was wearing the forbidding face she had seen in his study. There was no trace of kindness in him now. "Care for you? I care very much—for certain portions of you, that is. I have been without a willing woman for a long time, Miss Denham. You are not only young and beautiful, but you seem to be more than usually ripe for the picking.

"If you could be so kind as to lie on your back for me, for instance, I would most certainly be appreciative. I had thought my sad, tragic story would allow me to work my way into your bed. I had not counted on arousing your infantile affections as well. But, unfortunately, you are very immature, and prone to romantic exaggerations which could only complicate matters once I'd had my fill of you."

Another woman might have swooned. Another woman might have jumped up and beat furiously at him, hoping to return injury for injury, hurt for hurt. Yet another woman might have quietly acquiesced, willing to take him on his own terms.

Christine sat very still for a long time, allowing the tears to roll unchecked down her cheeks, not caring if he saw them. Then, just as the silence had grown nearly unbearable, she spoke, her voice very small in the huge chamber, caressing him with its tenderness, its compassion. "I suspect I might be falling in love with you too, Vincent."

Hawkhurst bolted out of the chair, nearly knocking Christine down as he reeled almost drunkenly toward the fireplace, quickly, prudently, putting half a room between them.

"What am I going to do with you, woman? Don't you listen? Don't you understand? I'm rejecting you, totally and absolutely. I don't want you. I don't want you here, in my house. I don't want you in my life. Damn you, Christine, why can't you leave me alone?"

Still on the floor, Christine turned her upper body, supporting herself on her hands as she stared at him as he was revealed in the firelight, glad to see that he was dressed in only breeches and an open-collared white shirt, with the cloak nowhere in evidence. She was stretching toward him, a supplicant, begging to be heard. "You would do this, Vincent? You would condemn us both?"

"Condemn us? What would I be condemning us to Christine? I would regain my hard-won peace, and you'd go off to London to enjoy a successful debut. The condemnation, my sweet infant, would be in allowing you to stay." His voice rose as his control threatened to snap. "I do not love you. I refuse to love you! Go now, Christine. Leave me with some shred of my dignity."

She did as he bid, rising, her shoulders bowed under the weight of her defeat, her humiliation, his complete and utter rejection of her. Shunning the dark passageway, she walked to the door, turning at the last moment to see him, still standing in front of the mantel, his head bent, massaging his left shoulder.

"I'm sorry for you, Vincent," she said, her voice breaking. "I'm so very sorry—for both of us."

FOURTEEN

Christine ran down the long hallway, nearly blinded by her tears, searching in her pocket for the key to her own bedchamber.

It took her an eternity to insert the key in the lock, an eternity during which she prayed that no servant would find it necessary to walk down the hallway. Finally, closing the door behind her, she gratefully leaned against it, her eyes squeezed tightly shut, her breast heaving, as she tried to recapture her breath.

Suddenly her eyelids slammed open. What was that sound? How could she have forgotten? The passageway. The sound had come from the passageway! Although in two separate rooms, she and Vincent were still linked together by the open passage. Her gaze quickly shifted to the paneling as she wildly wondered how she would ever be able to close it, but the wall was already sliding shut.

Her tears dried on her cheeks. "Vincent," she said unnecessarily into the empty air. He had closed off the corridor, sparing her the embarrassment of having to ask him to do it. She stood away from the door, slowly shaking her head. "Was it to help me, Vincent, I wonder, or am I still hopelessly trying to fashion an angel from a devil?"

Her mind whirled about, seeking another answer. Perhaps he had hurried to close the panel in order to show her just one more time how completely and utterly he wanted her out of his life.

"Well," she announced with a defiant toss of her dark curls, "I can only hope he didn't do himself an injury in his rush to seal the doorway. I shan't be tempted to use the passage again."

She busied herself for the next few minutes in moving the small tables back to their original positions around the chamber, blowing out at least half the candles she had lit earlier, her agile mind reliving the last half hour with varying results.

"As a matter of fact, it would be no great wonder to me if I were to be awakened bright and early tomorrow morning to the sound of Vincent's man Lazarus nailing the secret door shut with a dozen foot long spikes," she muttered, pushing the last table back into place with a none too gentle nudge from her hip.

Walking over to the window, she laid her forehead against the cold glass, hoping it would ease the headache now pounding behind her eyes. Outside, the world was dark, with only a faint moonlight etching weird patterns on the snow. The scene, once beautiful to her, now seemed barren and vaguely oppressive.

"Oh, what a fool I am, just as Vincent said. What a complete and utter ninnyhammer. Why, I all but fell at his feet, begging for him to love me. Aunt Nellis would have me locked up for life if she were to learn of it—immediately after she recovered from her nervous spasm, of course. Whatever possessed me to believe that Vincent might be falling in love with me? Or that I could be falling in love with him?"

She pulled the drapery closed and turned away from the window to begin unbuttoning the front closure of her gown, not caring when her trembling fingers succeeded in tearing one of the buttons from the fabric, to send it bouncing off into a dark corner.

"He's an awful, terrible man, that's what he is, a truly dreadful person. And he was right, I *was* weaving silly, romantic dreams around him. He's such a tragic figure, just the sort gullible young girls love to gush over. That's the only reason he told me his story. To gain my sympathy so he could use me. And yet, when I gave him his chance, he turned away from me."

Christine stepped out of her gown and tossed it carelessly onto a nearby chair, then began removing her chemise. She tilted her head to one side, recalling more of Vincent's words.

"Yet I *do* appeal to him. He told me so," she remembered, slightly comforted by the thought. It was so strange. She had always thought of beauty in terms of face and fashion. It hadn't occurred to her that her body could be a source of fascination.

Slowly, tentatively, she raised her hands to her breasts, then ran them experimentally over her body, sensing a new awareness of her physical form, a new yearning, a foreign hunger. She conjured up a mental picture of Vincent's body, the way his muscular firmness had felt as she had pressed her softness against him.

A shudder racked her body. "Oh, Vincent," she breathed on a sigh, reliving their impassioned kiss in the garden. "I'm so sorry!"

How she had tempted him in her innocence, her silly, juvenile stupidity! He was, after all, a man, with a man's yearnings. And she was a woman, feeling the first real stirrings of her womanhood.

Love, to Christine, had always meant holding hands, and kissing, and thinking sweet thoughts. This feeling, this sudden warmth mixed with mounting frustration, she knew without being told, was another side of love. This was loving. This was needing. This was wanting.

She willed her hands back to her sides.

"There seems to be a whole wealth of information Aunt Nellis has neglected to impart to me," she decided thoughtfully, quickly removing her remaining garments and nearly diving into the concealment of her heavy cotton nightgown.

She mounted the small wooden steps and crept onto the wide bed, sliding her feet under the covers to touch the now cold brass warmer. Her tears were back, silent tears that knew nothing of shame but much of understanding.

"Dearest Vincent," she whispered into the darkness. "How much you must love me, if you are willing to send me away."

Fifty feet. Not an insurmountable distance. It would take him less than half a minute to close the gap. Two doors. Just wood, easily disposed of by depressing the right triggers. No great barrier to keep him from what he wanted. No hindrance at all.

He raised his hand to hold it suspended six inches above the candle in the holder beside his chair. He couldn't feel the heat. But, if he lowered his hand, the heat would do more than warm him. It would burn him. If he could hold his hand three inches above the flame for a count of fifty, surely he would deserve a reward.

He closed his eyes and carefully lowered his hand until he could feel the heat radiating into his palm. "One . . . two . . . three . . ." he began, slowly counting the numbers out loud the way he had done so many times before in so many other private games meant to keep him from going insane. He barely noticed the discomfort.

". . . nine . . . ten . . . eleven . . ." The heat was beginning to penetrate his skin. Or was this madness itself, twisted around to make him think he was sane? Had his solitude finally served to unhinge him? Was he seriously considering such an asinine, juvenile stunt to be a game? Did he really believe he could use this trial by fire as justification for traveling down that fifty-foot-long passageway to claim Christine for his own?

He pulled his hand away, disgusted with himself, and flung his body back into the chair he had been sitting in, sulking in, when Christine had crept into his chamber. "I must be mad," he muttered, dropping his chin onto his chest as he glared into the fire.

The firelight danced over his sprawled figure, reflecting in his eyes, highlighting his flawed per-

fection, revealing his inner torment. He looked
into the flames, but he saw only Christine.
Christine, kneeling at his feet, her dark hair
tumbling away from that slight widow's peak to
flow down past her shoulders. Her sweet little
face registering her confusion, revealing all that
was in her heart, mirroring her loving soul.

There was no flaw in her, either hidden or
apparent. She was not a great work of art, to be
admired, or a paragon, to be placed on a pedestal
and worshiped from afar.

She was merely and supremely Christine.
Tenacious, playful, at times belligerent, not
without moments of temper, and more than a little
adventurous. These were not flaws, or faults. They
were just the wonderful facets that came together
to make Christine the lovely, desirable whole that
she was.

Why hadn't he seen that? Why hadn't he known?
Why had it taken him so long to understand?
Objects weren't perfect. Life wasn't perfect.
People weren't perfect. Perfection, beauty,
happiness was, is, in the eyes of the beholder.

Vincent sat stiffly forward, feeling that he was
on the verge of a great discovery.

Arabella. She had been so lovely, so very lovely.
She had been his dream, his ideal, walking into his
life to make his dreams reality.

"And when she couldn't live up to my perfect
dream of her," he said slowly, his words measured
as he tried to understand this horrifying
revelation, "she allowed that dream to destroy
her."

He was still guilty, he knew that, but he had

been suffering for all the wrong reasons. It wasn't that Arabella had been flawed, it was that he had made her believe she was flawed. She had been human, no more, no less. He had been human, no more, no less.

His sin wasn't that he had loved too much. His sin was that he had loved too little. He had fashioned an impossible ideal, a perfect happiness, and tried to mold Arabella to fit inside it.

A woman like Christine would have fought him.

A woman like Arabella had chosen another way out.

Vincent raised his hand to stroke the well-remembered scars on his face. He could still see them in his mind's eye, raised, and angrily red, and incredibly ugly—the outward signs of his guilt, his overweening arrogance, his damnable stupidity. His fingers came away wet, moistened by tears he hadn't been aware of shedding.

Everything was different, but nothing had changed. Arabella was still dead, and he was still responsible for that death. He did not deserve to be happy.

The following morning it snowed again, but only for a few hours. Later that day the sun returned to the land.

Outside the walls of Hawk's Roost, the thaw had begun.

FIFTEEN

Hawk's Roost wasn't an overlarge estate, as country estates went, even if it was the earl's oldest and primary seat. Its bedrooms didn't number in the hundreds, nor could the house boast elaborately hung state chambers reserved especially for visiting royalty.

It was a most charming place, rather than an impressive edifice; a single, tasteful jewel of mellowed pinkish brick and large expanses of glass, as opposed to a gaudy diamond necklace sporting turrets and sprawling wings in a hodgepodge of architectural styles.

It was, however, large enough to make it possible for a person wishing to avoid the presence of another person residing within the same walls to accomplish his purpose without difficulty. When two people were both of a mind to steer a wide course around each other, the task became downright simple.

Simple, that is, except for Lazarus, who seemed to be spending all his waking hours dashing back and forth between his master and the Misses Denham, trying to serve them all without acknowledging one's existence to the other. This was made doubly difficult thanks to Miss Nellis Denham, who seemed to have developed a near obsession with the absent earl.

"I shall never understand it," Aunt Nellis spoke up quickly as Lazarus entered the drawing room with the afternoon tea tray. "It is just the greatest mystery. The strangest thing, I vow, since the disappearance of those two poor, innocent boys in the Tower."

The servant rolled his eyes, for it appeared that the dratted woman was at it again. "Yes, ma'am, if you say so," he murmured dutifully, trying not to meet her eyes, which seemed determined to look straight through him. Of all the things Lazarus did not like about Nellis Denham, he liked her eyes least of all.

Aunt Nellis looked up as if surprised to find him there. "Oh, my, Lazarus," she exclaimed in a high voice, a hand fluttering to her breast. "I didn't see you come in. I was addressing my niece. I am sorry. You must be wondering what I was referring to, I'm sure, and thinking that my mind is breaking under the strain of our enforced sojourn here—I have at last taken to speaking nonsense."

"Of course, ma'am," the servant agreed, happy to be overlooked. "I mean," he added swiftly, realizing what he'd said, "it wasn't nonsense, I don't believe, but only that I, um, that is . . ."

"You were about to say something, Aunt Nellis, I believe?" Christine put in helpfully, for the afternoon was plodding along on leaden feet and she thought her aunt might be about to lend some slight diversion to the long hours. She wasn't to be disappointed.

"Yes, yes, I was, thank you, dearest Christine. It has been over a week since his lordship invited us to dine with him and then sent his regrets at the last minute," the older woman pointed out for what had to be the fiftieth time in ten days. "It begs the question, you know. *Why* hasn't he made an appearance?"

"Perhaps he is unsure as to which fork to use and does not wish to open himself to ridicule," Christine said, wishing her aunt would move on to another subject. She was looking for diversion. She had more than enough reminders of Vincent Mayhew's determined avoidance of her without her aunt's dredging his name into the conversation every second minute.

Aunt Nellis went on, undaunted by her niece's mild sarcasm. "He was looking quite odd that first evening, you know, Christine. I'm sure, now that I look back on it, that he must have been sickening for something. That would explain his hiding himself away, wouldn't it?"

"Lazarus has assured me that the earl is not ill, Aunt," Christine said wearily to save time, still standing at the long window where she had spent most of the afternoon watching the snow melt.

Aunt Nellis sniffed dismissively. "Of course he would, my dear. After all, he's in the man's employ."

"And what does that have to do with anything?" Christine asked, knowing her aunt would tell her, whether she wished for the information or nay.

More important to her was the thaw taking place outside.

She watched as a heavily loaded branch swayed in a slight breeze, then shed its mantle of snow onto the ground. Already there were high spots of winter-brown grass visible in the distance. Soon there would be no excuse for remaining at Hawk's Roost. Then what would she do? Would he really let her go without ever meeting with her again?

"What does it have to do with anything?" Aunt Nellis repeated, aghast. "Why, it has everything to do with it, of course! Don't you understand, Christine? The earl could be ill with some horribly contagious disease." Her voice filled with horror. "Possibly even the *plague*! And we've both been exposed to contagion!"

Lazarus was stung into speech. "Of all the silly, shatter-brained—"

"Lazarus!" Christine interposed quickly, knowing the servant was about to make a muck of things. "Didn't I just hear a bell in the distance? I do believe the earl requires your presence. We're fine here, and it wouldn't do to keep him waiting."

"Yes, miss, of course," Lazarus said hastily, throwing her a grateful look before scurrying out of the room, cravenly fleeing the scene of his near insubordination as Nellis Denham glared impotently after him. She had so counted on the man's help, but he had proved to be a dead loss.

"The plague, Aunt?" Christine scolded once the servant was gone. "Really, I do believe you are allowing your imagination to get the better of you."

"Well, he could be," Aunt Nellis grumbled,

picking up her teacup. She focused all her attention now on her main target, her niece. "And don't be so smug. You didn't see him that first evening, all wrapped in that cloak. I've been giving it a lot of thought, and he could be hiding his face —so that we can't see the ugly pox, the running sores. Why, he could be dead, for all we know!"

Christine sat down on a chair facing her aunt and picked up her own teacup, willing her hands not to shake. Her aunt had set her mind to racing. Could Vincent really be ill? She hadn't thought of that. Yet aloud, she said, "You can hide a multitude of things in the countryside, Aunt Nellis, but I doubt that you can keep a dead earl a secret for very long. Please pass me that plate. Those cheese sandwiches look very appetizing."

Aunt Nellis did as she was bid, then remained leaning forward, her protuberant hazel eyes narrowed. She pushed on, willing to try anything to achieve her end. "I don't *really* believe the earl is ailing, Christine," she admitted conspiratorially, winking at her niece. 'I was only trying to surprise Lazarus into spilling the truth, but you innocently thwarted me there."

"The truth?" Christine repeated hollowly, beginning to believe she had underestimated her aunt's propensity for imaginative thinking. "What truth?"

Aunt Nellis looked first left, then right, as if she were making sure no one had secreted themselves in the room in order to overhear anything she might have to say. She lowered her voice a full octave, saying importantly, "I think there's something very havey-cavey about our absent host,

Christine, my dear. As a matter of fact—*I don't believe he's an earl at all!*"

"Not—not an earl?" Unaware that, for the most part, she had spent the past few minutes doing little more than repeating anything her aunt had said, Christine frowned, trying to understand this latest flight of fancy. "Then—then what is he, if he's not the Earl of Hawkhurst?"

Aunt Nellis's eyes were narrow slits, her expression cunning in the extreme. "*He's a murderer!*" she whispered excitedly, feeling she had at last hit on the perfect, if slightly melodramatic, tack.

Christine felt her face pale. Her Aunt Nellis knew? How could she know? "A murderer?"

Her aunt nodded vigorously, the bit firmly between her teeth as she saw she had her niece's full attention. "He's killed the real earl and now he's taking his place. He uses Hawk's Roost as the center of his highwayman activities, riding out under cover of darkness to murder innocent people traveling the highways, then returning here to play the innocent, reclusive nobleman, with nobody the wiser. That's why he met me that first night still wearing a cloak. He had just returned from one of his bloody expeditions. We're sharing a house with a *murderer*! Think on it, Christine. It fits. It all fits!"

Relief raced through Christine's body, making her want to giggle. She slowly lowered her teacup to the table, then sat back to stare, wide-eyed, at the now widely grinning woman. "Aunt Nellis," she said, tight-lipped, "I think you've been snowbound too long."

Her aunt instantly bristled. "I would appreciate it, Christine, if you would refrain from making fun of me. I'm deadly serious."

"Yes, I know," Christine answered, at last unable to hold back her laughter. "That's what makes it so funny. The earl is a highwayman. Really, Aunt. What would he possibly find on the road that he doesn't possess in abundance right here? This house is a virtual treasure trove."

Aunt Nellis leaned forward even further, putting one tip of her paisley shawl in danger of dangling into her teacup. It was now or never, and hang the consequences! "Adventure, Christine," she breathed, her expression avid. "Excitement." Her features flattened. "Rapine—pillage."

For the first time in her life Christine hated her aunt. How dare she accuse gentle Vincent of such things! Her palms itched from the urge to reach out and slap the animalistic look from the woman's face.

"No! How dare you! He isn't anything like that! He's good, and kind, and decent!" she shouted, jumping to her feet to return to the window, placing her back to Aunt Nellis as she wrapped her arms about herself, shaking in her fury.

Behind her, Aunt Nellis dropped her head into her hands, silently begging Christine's forgiveness, yet knowing she had been proved correct. She had seen the looks that had been traded back and forth between her niece and Lazarus, noticed the quick cessation of whispered conversations between them as she entered a room. Christine had been acting oddly ever since the coach accident, and these drastic changes couldn't all be attributed to a simple bang on the head.

The girl had been with the mysterious earl, Aunt Nellis was now thoroughly convinced of it. Christine had seen him, talked with him, met him behind her aunt's back, defying every principle of correct behavior that Nellis Denham had spent her life instilling in her.

The older woman wrung her hands in an agony of hurt and indecision, not knowing what to do next. Should she confront her niece with what she knew? Should she keep her own counsel, especially since she was sure that whatever relationship the earl and Christine had had, it was over now? If nothing else, she could thank the earl for his belated good sense. Still, should she, could she, stand back and watch as Christine continued to curl in on herself, her unhappiness a tangible thing?

They had to get away from here, to London, as soon as possible.

Aunt Nellis silently cursed the weather, that was taking its own sweet time ridding the landscape of snow, only to replace it with foot-deep mud that would clog the highways for at least another week.

She likewise cursed the mysterious earl, who had dared to lead her niece into possible scandal and probable heartbreak.

She had to get Christine shed of this place, of this man, before they destroyed her.

Slowly, feeling all the weight of her years, Nellis Denham rose and walked across the room to stand behind her niece. "Christine," she said softly, gently, touching her hand to Christine's back, "he isn't for you. He knows it. Now you must accept it."

"Oh, Aunt Nellis!" Christine wailed, turning about to throw her arms around her aunt, who clasped her tightly against her comforting bosom. "I love him. I love him so much!"

SIXTEEN

Vincent watched in silent wonderment as the fingers of his left hand slowly moved upward in his lap, curling around the white queen. The fingers didn't quite touch the wood, but they were even closer to that point tonight than they had been yesterday. If his improvement was this marked after only ten days of exercise, within another week he should be able to make a fist.

"Amazing," he marveled, unaware of the beads of perspiration standing out on his brow, or the tightness of his straining muscles, uncaring that this particular feat had taken him twenty minutes of physical agony and all his concentration.

Removing the chess piece with his right hand, he stood, ready to face the next test. Walking over to stand a foot away from the wall, he pushed his left arm out toward the wall by shifting the muscles on his left side.

The arm moved stiffly, as if it were not really a part of him at all, but on the third attempt the knuckles on the back of his hand touched against the wall and held there, as the pain in his damaged

shoulder threatened to send him crashing to his
knees.

He took a deep breath and commanded his
fingers to begin crawling up the wall, first by
moving one finger, then the next, in awkward
imitation of the spider he had seen climbing there
that had given him the idea for this exercise in the
first place.

His progress was measured in quarter inches,
his elbow bending slowly, his left side pushing
forward to help in the ascent as his shoulder
muscles screamed in protest. He stood on tiptoe as
the pain shot through him, searching for release
from the unbearable tenseness, the shrunken
muscles in his upper arm and chest feeling like
taut bands that were being stretched to the point
of snapping.

He stopped, his fingers now almost elbow high,
and took another deep breath, knowing that
lowering his arm would prove to be as painful a
journey as raising it had been. But he had gone at
least an inch higher than he had that afternoon
and, although its slowness was infuriating, he was
making progress. Only last week he had been
unable to touch the wall at all, his left arm only
swinging against his side like a badly hung garden
gate in a fall breeze.

Returning to the chair before the fire, he sank
into it gratefully, no longer furious with himself
for his exhaustion. His only anger was that he had
waited this long to try to regain the use of his arm.
The signs had been there for a long time, the
physical evidence that his arm had not been
rendered totally useless by Fletcher's muscle

slashing whip, but he had not wanted to acknowledge this silent forgiveness for his great sin.

For nearly two months after his beating, Vincent's left arm had been made totally immobile —tied tightly against his body in a sling to keep his wounds from reopening—even on the day he was told that he had become the seventh Earl of Hawkhurst.

When the sling and the bandages had finally been removed, the arm was, in his bitterly uttered words, "fit only to serve as a tolerable paper-weight." He had completely ignored his doctor's plea to try to restore the arm's strength by means of simple exercise, choosing instead to hide himself away at Hawk's Roost where he could wallow alone in his misery.

Looking back on those first terrible months, the inactivity had served only to worsen his problem, he was sure of that now. The muscles in his back, in his chest—muscles that had once been honed to near perfection by his active, sports-filled life-style—had paid the price of his perverted martyrdom, and they were rebelling most boisterously now at even the most simple commands.

Vincent reached over to pick up the brandy snifter that stood on the table beside his chair and drained its contents in one long gulp, then leaned back in his chair and smiled. He couldn't help it. He was proud of himself—proud of his achieve-ment.

Christine would be proud of him too if only she could see him. He would perform his little party tricks for her and she would jump up and down, clap her hands delightedly and exclaim, "Oh, Vincent, how wonderful!" before racing over to throw her arms about his neck and kiss him firmly on the mouth.

The smile slowly faded. "Christine," he said aloud, missing her more than even he—the man who had purposely sent her away—had thought possible.

For more than four years he had cherished his solitude, neither wanting nor needing company. He had found some measure of peace. He had almost begun to believe he could look at himself, look at his life, and not miss the old Vincent or the life that had been before.

Now he was as frustrated as the lions he had seen pacing their small cages at country fairs, his leashed energy threatening to explode at any moment, the urge to roar and howl nearly too compelling to be ignored. He refused to go outside, not wanting to chance seeing Christine and thereby having to say good-bye to her again. So, like the jungle cats, he prowled the cage of his study hour after hour, day after day, free to roam only as he slept, fitfully, his body never really at rest, his mind never finding real peace.

He had thought and thought, rationalized and agonized, as Lazarus hovered over him fretfully, begging him to eat, to rest, to stop his constant demands on his injured body. At last, he had come to a decision so startling, so cleansing, so alien to all his thoughts of so many years, that he had fallen into his chair and wept.

The past was the past! Yes, he had done wrong.

He had been younger then, full of himself and his grand ideals and ideas of the world. His picture of life had been distorted, a young man's dream of perfection, colored perhaps by his own physical appearance and his then seemingly charmed life.

Arabella's tragic death had shattered that dream in an instant, and Fletcher's devastating revenge had stripped him of his fairy-tale life.

Strangely, his altered physical appearance had also ceased to bother him. Christine hadn't recoiled from him. Oh yes, she had screamed that first night she'd seen him, but he had managed to rationalize that occurrence away. She had been riding along in a coach, on her way to London, only to suddenly find herself awakening, injured, in a strange bed, with a strange man hovering over her. Her frightened screams had been pure reaction.

He didn't like his scars, still thought them ugly, still hadn't garnered the courage to look at them, but he could live with them if she could.

He had even stopped believing that they were the outward sign of his shame. They were scars, nothing more, nothing less, at least to him. The concealing cloaks he had favored for so long had been put away, and he would not wear them again.

The only thing he could not see himself ever doing was making a return to London. That part of his life was over.

But that didn't mean that his entire life was over! He had been to the brink—and possibly a bit beyond—but now he was on his way back, to life, to sanity, to hope for the future. Christine was bringing him back from the edge, whether she was

in his arms or out of his life forever. She didn't
know it, but she had saved his life. If he never saw
her again he would always be grateful to her.

She was suffering, his darling girl. Lazarus had
taken special care to tell him that, and the
knowledge pained Vincent even as it cheered him.
She loved him, or at least she thought she did. Yet
she knew little of life, hidden away at Manderley
with only that rather strange aunt to guide her.

Vincent had to stand back and let Christine have
her Season. He had to allow her a taste of life
outside the shadows, and pray that she wouldn't
forget him once she was in the glittering world of
London. He had to allow her to hear the story of
his disgrace, his heartbreak, from the people she
would meet, and to make her own decisions as to
his guilt or innocence.

Only then could he invite her back to visit him at
Hawk's Roost.

And he would go slowly with her even then. He
wouldn't make the same mistakes he had made
with Arabella, forcing his love on her before she
was ready to receive it.

His only worry was, even if she still loved him,
could he really ask her to live here with him,
secluded forever at Hawk's Roost, away from
Society, where his scars wouldn't be a constant
source of whispers and reminders of his past? For,
as far as he had come, he had not come far enough
to be ready to face the London *ton*, even with a
loving Christine on his arm. It would bring it all
back, when he was ready at last to forget it. He
couldn't subject Christine to the scandal his
appearance would always provoke.

So, he would have to wait, and hope, and believe

that Christine truly loved him, and that her love would bring her back to him.

"And when she comes, if she comes," he said aloud, watching as once more his left hand strained to close around the white queen, "I shall hold her close in both my arms and never, *ever* let her go again."

SEVENTEEN

"Come, Christine," Aunt Nellis urged fretfully, heading for the front door, a red and white striped bandbox banging against her hip as she walked, "we've tarried long enough. The coachman Lazarus engaged for us in the village told me he hopes to make Paddock Wood before nightfall, and that's twelve miles from here at the least. Thank heaven that other man took his repaired coach and moved on yesterday. I would rather walk to London than ride with him again!"

"Yes, Aunt," Christine answered dutifully, slowly making her way down the broad staircase, a similar bandbox in her own hand. "You go on without me. I just want to say good-bye to Cook, and then I'll join you in the coach."

"Say good-bye to the cook?" Aunt Nellis asked, looking puzzled for a moment before biting her lip and resignedly nodding her head. "Oh, yes, yes. The cook, of course. He was very kind, wasn't he? He has even packed some sandwiches for us to eat on the way. Go along then, dear, but please don't be long. Who knows if this fine weather will hold."

"Thank you, Aunt Nellis," Christine said gratefully, standing very straight on the bottom step, her chin resolutely held high. The day she had dreaded had finally arrived, without so much as a single word or nocturnal visit from Vincent. Was he going to allow her to walk out of his life without even saying good-bye? Was he actually planning to let their last, horrible meeting be the memory she would take away with her?

"Well," Christine said with conviction, carelessly tossing aside the bandbox containing her aunt's second-best bonnet, "as I remember the saying, 'it is a bad plan that admits of no modification.' There are times when it takes a woman to do what must be done, and *this* is most definitely one of those times!"

Letting go of the newel post she had been clinging to as if it was the only support keeping her from tumbling into a yawning abyss, Christine descended the final step and turned toward the door to Vincent's study. As she crossed the black and white tiled foyer, her jean half boots kicking against her heavy skirts, her pace increased until, without bothering to knock, she flung open the study door so that it slammed loudly against the inside wall and burst into the room.

"Vincent? *Vincent!* I'm going now," she announced baldly, her gaze avidly searching the room for some sign of him. "I know you love me. Are you really fool enough to let me go?"

"I'd be twice the fool to let you stay, imp. You are fast destroying my property as well as my best intentions. I have just come back from saying my farewells to your aunt in hopes of finding you."

He was here! Hawkhurst's words had come

from behind her, and Christine whirled about, startled, to see him standing in the doorway, smiling down at her. It was full daylight and Vincent was standing bareheaded, his scars totally revealed. He looked wonderful, devilishly handsome despite his imperfections, and very much at his ease.

There was so much she wanted to say to him! "Vincent! You—you're not wearing your cloak," she heard herself saying stupidly.

"Yes, I had noticed that, especially once I had stepped outside onto the drive. You'll need your muff, I fear. I have already entrusted it to your aunt. Now, good morning, dearest girl," he went on most congenially as she continued to stare up at him, open-mouthed. "Oh, dear, what's wrong? Have you forgotten what you were going to say? I think it had something to do with calling me a fool. There's really no need. I know I am. Can you ever forgive me for the terrible things I said the night you came to my room?"

Christine's heart skipped a beat as she devoured him with her eyes. It was suddenly the most beautiful morning the world had ever known. Oh, how she loved him, how she had missed him. She slipped easily back into their banter, as if that last evening had never happened.

"Of course I forgive you! But, for nearly two weeks you have been avoiding me, only to appear as if conjured up by a magician just as I am about to leave. Not only that—why are you being so nice? I mean, to go to my aunt, to let her see you. I don't understand. It is totally out of character for a mysterious recluse."

"I can't believe I have actually missed that sharp tongue of yours." Vincent took hold of her elbow, guiding her further into the study. "Your aunt and I have spoken several times in the past few days, Christine," Vincent told her, only confusing her more. "She's a very nice woman, if a bit imaginative. She's been putting poor Lazarus through hoops ever since she arrived."

Christine shook her head. "Aunt Nellis never told me," she said, almost to herself. "She's never been able to keep a secret. *Never*." She looked up at Hawkhurst, her sky-blue eyes suddenly filled with tears. "Why her, Vincent? Why her, and not me?"

Vincent ignored her question, only reaching into his pocket to extract an oblong velvet box that he pressed into her hand. "I wanted to give this to you before you left. Will you wear it some time, and perhaps think of me?"

Christine opened the box with trembling fingers, a silent gasp escaping her lips as she looked down on a pearl necklace of such simple perfection that she couldn't quite believe it was real. She raised her head to look at him, seeing the quick pain in his eyes before he had a chance to hide his emotions behind an impersonal smile.

"Thank you, Vincent," she said quietly. "I'll wear it always."

Vincent nodded his approval, looking toward the hallway. "You have to go now if you wish to make much progress before stopping for the night. The coachman told me the roads still aren't very fit for traveling."

Christine stood her ground, a horrifying

thought having just sprung into her mind. "These pearls—are these your way of saying good-bye? If they are, I don't want them. I could never bear to look at them."

Reaching out his hand to softly stroke the back of his knuckles against her cheek, Vincent said gently, "Not good-bye. Never good-bye. You will always be in my heart."

She reached up, trapping his hand against her face. He was so dear to her, so necessary to her. "Then why, Vincent? Why are you making me go? Don't you know you're tearing me apart?"

His eyes were bleak as they looked at her. "I know, my dearest, I know. But I must allow you your Season. I must allow you to learn more about me than your own romantic notions of this strange, reclusive earl who gave you shelter from the storm. I must force you back into the world, the world I have chosen to leave behind, so that you can be sure of what you want. Please allow me to believe that at least I have learned from my mistakes."

"A Season! That's my aunt's wish, not mine. It was never mine. I know what I want, Vincent," Christine argued, wrapping her arms tightly around him, pressing her head against his chest. "Please, don't listen to my aunt. Don't send me away. I love you!"

Tipping her head up by placing a finger beneath her chin, Vincent stared at her for a long time, as if trying to memorize every feature of her face. "Please, Christine, don't make this parting any more difficult for us than it already is. Please, go now."

"Aren't—aren't you even going to kiss me before I go?" Her voice cracked with heartbreak.

. Vincent smiled ruefully, shaking his head. "I have been many things, Christine, in the course of my lifetime. But one thing I have finally learned is that I am a complete failure in the role of martyr. No, my darling girl, I will not kiss you. I can't."

"Then will you come to London sometime, to visit me?" she asked, already knowing the answer but, like a child attempting to find some way to get what she wanted even after it had been made clear to her that it was impossible, she would try anything. But when she saw the bleakness in his eyes she relented. "Oh, Vincent, forgive me. It's your scars, isn't it? But they don't matter now. You're not even wearing that horrible cloak anymore."

"At Hawk's Roost my scars no longer matter. In London, they are everything," he explained, his eyes sad. "As you will doubtless learn before long if I can trust your dearest aunt to ferret out the gossip, and I'm sure I can."

Christine knew what he meant, but she also knew it was fruitless to argue with him. He had made up his mind. He was going to send her away, believing that the social round of London and the scandal she was sure to hear about would serve to make her forget him, or even despise him.

He was wrong, he was so wrong, and she had to convince him. But how? Words meant so little. And there had already been too many words. It was only action that would prove anything to him now.

"I'll go, Vincent, as you want me to," she told

him just before she stood on tiptoe and pressed her lips to his before he had a chance to move away from her. Her heart was in her kiss, her love for him eloquently, wordlessly expressed. Her fingers spread against his chest, then slid upward to clasp his shoulders, her mouth opening beneath his as his heart gave him no choice but to take what she had offered.

He flung his right arm about her and drew her hard against him one last time, the two of them communicating silently, their simmering passion allowed this fleeting moment of freedom. Then Christine slowly pushed herself away from him.

"I'll not change my mind, Vincent," she told him, her voice steady, her course at last certain. "I will always love you. But I will not come to you here at the end of the Season as proof of my affections. You are not the only one to be laying down conditions for our love. If you love me, really love me, you will have to come to me in London. I won't let you keep hiding from the world."

Vincent stiffened. "I can't come to London, Christine. It would bring back all the old hurts. I can't punish Fletcher that way, for one thing, and I don't want to hurt you."

"Fletcher?" Christine wrinkled her brow, trying to understand. "Oh, I think I know. Fletcher is the man who beat you, isn't he? Do you think he would try something else? He wouldn't dare!"

"No," Vincent answered shortly. "He's had sufficient time for a dozen acts of revenge. I just don't want to bring back all his painful memories of his sister, and my face, my very presence, would do that. And then the tongues would begin to wag all over again. He's been hurt enough. I can't go to London, even for you, Christine."

Christine's control broke. "I hate this man Fletcher! I hate him!" she said fervently, her small hands drawn up into tight fists.

"Don't hate him, Christine. Fletcher Belden is a good man."

"Then I hate what he's done to you. Surely I'm allowed that? Why can't you tell me what happened to his sister if you feel it is so important that I know? Don't you see, it doesn't matter. Nothing matters. I love you!"

Vincent's smile was sad. "Yet we have both put conditions on that love, haven't we? I once told you that love was the greatest sin a person could commit. I had begun to think I was wrong. Now I am not so sure."

"Vincent, I—"

"Go, Christine, have your Season," he interrupted, taking her elbow once more and purposefully leading her toward the doorway. "In June, when the last snow is only a memory, we will meet again, somehow, some way, I promise. And your aunt has agreed to it, at least for now."

Christine turned to him one last time, pressing her hand against his chest, to make one last plea. "Will you at least say it? Will you at least give me something to take with me on this terrible journey to London?"

Vincent didn't have to ask what she meant. "I love you, Christine," he said, his voice little more than a hoarse whisper. "I love you."

And then he was gone, leaving her to climb

aboard the coach with only Lazarus to help her, carefully avoiding her aunt's eyes as she curled herself into the far corner, her head rocking listlessly against the cushions as the servant gave the order to "Spring 'em."

EIGHTEEN

London

Nellis Denham believed the narrow rented house in Half Moon Street to be perfectly wonderful.

Christine Denham couldn't have cared if the house had been located atop a dung hill.

"Well, maybe I would have taken exception to *that*," Christine conceded grudgingly, wrinkling her nose as she sat curled in the window seat that overlooked the street, determined to maintain her miserable mood.

She had been in legendary Londontown for over a fortnight, and her mood had shifted from sorrowful to pettish—or at least that's what her aunt had told her before daringly going off to Bond Street with the newly employed maid, Harriet, in tow, leaving her stubborn niece in the care of the cook who had been hired at the same time.

Ernestine Flam, a very large, beefy woman

whose idea of service had a lot to do with having her own meals available hourly but little to do with being at anyone else's beck and call, had retired to the small kitchen on the ground floor the moment the door had closed on Aunt Nellis's back, leaving Christine to her own devices.

Christine had immediately repaired to the second-floor window seat, a handy vantage point from which she could glare down at the passersby while silently condemning them all for not being the Earl of Hawkhurst, come to declare his undying love.

How she hated this city, this house, this room, this bleak existence! And how, she thought, feeling slightly embarrassed, she had made her aunt suffer for it.

She hadn't spoken to the older woman all the way to London—not a single word—which wasn't easily done, as the trip had taken them a full three days to accomplish. At first she had been too upset, too brokenhearted, to utter a word. However, once she'd had time to remember that Nellis had spoken with Vincent while she, suffering silently, had been kept in the dark about it, Christine had allowed herself to build up quite a grudge against her devious though most probably well-intentioned aunt.

But when the woman had been so foolish as to complain, quite vocally, on their very first stop, that Christine had purposely forgotten her second-best bonnet at Hawk's Roost, Christine's anger had known no bounds.

That anger had sustained her, keeping her from remembering that it had been Vincent, and not her aunt, who had banished her from Hawk's Roost.

"And all for a silly Season in London," she complained, shaking her head. She looked down at the street again, seeing the dirt and disorder and the multitude of nameless, faceless people rushing hither and thither like ants hurriedly preparing for a long winter. "Why should anyone in their right mind ever miss this? London has all the charm of a pigsty."

It was true that Christine hadn't actually seen London at her loud, sprawling best. The Season was not fully upon the city, so that few of the really fashionable people, showing off their furs and feathers and finery, were out and about as yet. The hard winter had also taken its toll, and the muddy roadways into London had been clogged with overloaded drays and merchantmen eager to get their wares to market.

The houses their coach had passed were stained all over with chimney soot, while ashes seemingly ankle-deep were scattered about the flagways that overlooked the clogged gutters. Half-naked children, their feet wrapped in rags, had run alongside the coach, begging for pennies, while the smell of horse manure and burning meat pies seeped beneath the doors to assault Christine's nose.

Even the sight of St. Paul's, barely visible in the descending twilight and ascending fog, had done little to make Christine believe that her coming Season could be any more palatable than a visit to the tooth drawer.

"It will look better to you as soon as the weather clears," her aunt had assured her, and Christine had turned her head to hide a bitter smile, remembering an Aunt Nellis more used to portending doom than delight.

"I'll never forget the summer our roses were so outstandingly beautiful," Christine said out loud, using her forefinger to smear small circles on the windowpane, her mind traveling back to that pleasant, innocent time when she had never heard of Vincent Mayhew.

The entire garden had been glorious that year, with the roses particularly plentiful and hardy, but Aunt Nellis, ever one to see the storm clouds behind every rainbow, had fretted and fussed over each and every bloom, sure that disaster was hovering just outside the garden walls, ready to strike at the lovely flowers.

"It will probably rain for a week, rotting those new buds right on their branches," she had prophesied darkly in early June.

"This August sun is far too hot. We've seen the last good rose this summer, Christine," she had vowed as they sat on the stone bench in the early evening, admiring the latest crop of glorious blooms.

"I understand dear Sir Algernon Balderfield's roses have been devastated by a blight," Aunt Nellis had informed her niece over a bowl of fragrant yellow roses as they breakfasted on the terrace one morning in September. "Ours will surely be next."

And in late October, with the nip of autumn in the air, as Christine lowered her head to sniff at the heady fragrance of a flawless blood-red rose, Aunt Nellis had uttered the final, damning prophesy, "Yes, they're fine now—but wait until the beetles come!"

Christine's shoulders shook with mirth as she remembered her aunt's words, but her laughter stopped as a tall, cloaked figure alighted from a carriage onto the flagway. "Vincent!" she gasped, pressing both palms against the windowpane. "Oh, Vincent, you've come for me!"

She watched as he stood looking up and down the street, holding her breath, silently directing him to her door. He took a step in the right direction, then turned to walk the other way, stopping to mount front steps a set of two doors further down the street.

"No, no! You've got the wrong house," she cried, hitting her fist against the glass. "Not there! I'm here, Vincent, I'm here!"

A moment later the man reappeared, with another gentleman beside him, to return to the carriage. As they walked along, the tall man threw back his head to laugh at something his friend had said and his hood slid away, to reveal a full head of blond hair.

"Oh, Vincent," Christine groaned, pressing her forehead against the glass in defeat, tears stinging her eyes. "How my life has changed. It seems that all I have left to do now is sit here, waiting for Aunt Nellis's beetles."

A log split in the fireplace, crashing down into the grate in a shower of sparks, waking the Earl of Hawkhurst from his reverie. He looked around the study, trying to concentrate.

"What day is it, Lazarus?"

The servant looked up from his polishing to peer questioningly at his master. "Why, it's Tuesday, your lordship," he answered, unable to believe the man didn't know something as simple as that.

"No, no," Hawkhurst corrected. "I mean, what date is it? I seem to have lost track."

Lazarus held up the small brass, full-bottomed vase and huffed a breath of warm air at it, then attacked the piece with his polishing cloth. "Oh, that, sir. It's the fifteenth of March, I believe. Yes, that's it, because yesterday was my cousin's birthday, and that's always been on the fourteenth. You might wish to take a walk in the garden before I serve luncheon, sir. There's a hint of spring in the air outside."

Christine had been gone for nearly a month. Strange, he thought, frowning. It seemed longer than that. A lifetime. "Are you going to be much longer, Lazarus? I'd like to get started on my exercises."

"A few minutes, at most, your lordship," the servant replied, setting the vase back in its appointed place. "You'll be wanting the rope again today, sir?"

Vincent nodded, rising to begin the exercises he could do without waiting for Lazarus's assistance. Walking over to the side of the room, he put his left hand out confidently, knowing his fingertips would have no trouble finding purchase against the wall. He watched as his fingers climbed the wall, his elbow barely bending as his hand reached straight out as it climbed, his fingertips nearly shoulder high before the pain hit him, before his shoulder and chest muscles did their best to tie themselves into knots.

He was doing well, but he had to do so much better. Sometimes he could live with his slow recovery but other times, times like this, he wanted to curse the fates for his snail-like progress.

Yes, he had come a long way from those first awful days, when it had taken everything in him just to hold the back of his hand against this same wall and use the knuckles of his clawlike hand to elevate his arm the pitiful distance of three inches. Another man might have been satisfied with this increased achievement, even proud. Vincent was only growing more impatient with every passing day. He wanted, he needed, more.

"Here's the rope, your lordship. Are you sure you want me to do this again? I really don't like to, sir. It seems to hurt you so much."

"You're a good friend, Lazarus," Hawkhurst told the man, taking one end of the three-foot-long rope and transferring it to his left hand. He wrapped the rope twice around his hand to help secure it, then walked over to where Lazarus was already clambering up on top of a low stool. "Take the other end and begin to pull it up. Gently now, Lazarus, for I wouldn't wish to unman myself by crying out in front of you."

Lazarus took the end the earl held out to him and slowly began raising it, up, up, until his hand was higher than his head. As he raised the rope Vincent's arm lifted with it, first straight out in front of him, and then slightly higher. As he felt the first hint of resistance, the servant stopped, only to have his master urge him on. "Higher, man, higher. Lift my arm higher before you lower the rope. All right, now again. Lift it again."

Vincent's arm was raised and lowered, past the point of his shoulder, his muscles screaming as they were stretched as they hadn't been in nearly five years. It was a painful exercise, repeated six or more times a day, but it was the only thing Vincent could think of to help limber up his muscles. He couldn't lift his arm on his own. He would be performing the exercise ten times a day, a dozen, if Lazarus had not dared to put his foot down and refuse to help him.

The rope was raised ten more times before Hawkhurst signaled that he'd had enough, but he wasn't done. Relieving Lazarus of the rope, he let the free end drop, then stepped on it with his left foot. He held his arm out as straight as possible and then lifted it up until the rope was taut, pulling on it with all his might, trying to stretch it. The veins on his neck stood out, his scars burned like white hot brands on his face. Lazarus turned away, not wanting to watch his master in such obvious agony.

"Terrible, isn't it?" Vincent quipped through gritted teeth. "I have less strength than a babe in arms. But it won't always be like this. With your help, Lazarus, this arm is going to come back to life, whether it wants to or not. Remember, Rome wasn't built in a day."

"Yes, your lordship," the servant agreed sadly, picking up his polishing cloth before heading for the door. "But then this Rome place didn't have Miss Christine Denham to consider, did it?"

Vincent stopped trying to stretch the rope, allowing it to slip through his fingers, onto the floor. "Miss Denham knows nothing about this, Lazarus," he said, puzzled. "Oh, wait a moment. Did you think she rejected me because of my arm, and that I'm going through this hell only to please her? To try to win her?"

Lazarus hung his head, avoiding Hawkhurst's eyes. "Yes, sir. I did, sir."

"And here I've been thinking that you were a bright fellow, Lazarus," Vincent chided, shaking his head.

Fearful that his lordship was angry, the servant rushed into speech. "I know she's a very nice woman, your lordship, or at least she always was to me, even if her aunt is a bit queer, and I know that it's because of her being so nice that you've given off wearing those cloaks and going about Hawk's Roost only at night like a damned owl—I mean . . ."

"No, no, don't stop now," Vincent prompted, clearly intrigued by the man's free speech. "Please, go on. We've passed the point of servant and master these past few weeks. Speak to me as a friend, Lazarus. I find I have much need of friends."

For a few moments Lazarus seemed to consider whether or not his lordship could be taken at his word. The Quality were a strange bunch, he knew that from his past experiences, and not unlikely to be sweet as pie to him one minute, just to throw him out for insubordination the next, and without so much as a reference. But in the end, he yielded to his desire to speak.

"It's just that Miss Denham left here in a mighty huff, your lordship and there's not been note nor letter since. The way I figure it, she decided she couldn't deal with you the way you are, even if you two were getting, um, rather fond of each other. I didn't like that she left you that way, your lordship," he ended solemnly. "But women, especially pretty women like Miss Denham, can be fickle as the very devil!"

Walking across the room to put his arm around Lazarus's shoulders, Vincent told him, "You say Miss Denham left here in a huff, my friend. You are only half right. To be truthful, I threw her out. It was the only way she would go. She couldn't care less if I had one good arm or three. She thinks she loves me, poor darling. She has nothing to do with why I'm killing myself this way—or at least she doesn't have everything to do with it. I'm doing this for me, Lazarus, because I want to do it. Do you understand now?"

Lazarus looked up into his friend's face, Hawkhurst's words pleasing him. "I understand now, your lordship," he said, grinning. "You love her too!"

NINETEEN

Aunt Nellis had vowed sorrowfully again and again that it could never be done. It was impossible. There was no conceivable way she could have her dearest niece Christine ("Why, yes, dear Lady Wentworth, that's my brother's girl—the pretty, dark-haired one over there, sulking by herself in the corner") knocked into shape in time for opening night at Almack's.

Or could she?

Two cherished vouchers for this exalted bastion of eligibility had been procured through an old friend's sister-in-law's nephew, who had at some earlier time run tame in one of the patronesses' country houses, and although it had cost Aunt Nellis dearly in terms of her small store of favors owed she felt the expense would have been fair at twice the price.

But did Christine appreciate this gargantuan sacrifice? Did she understand that she had been singled out as one of the few, the very few, deemed important enough to be allowed to sip warm lemonade and eat stale cakes alongside the cream of the London *haut ton*?

Did she fall on her dearest aunt's neck in unbridled delight, raining kisses on her while profusely proclaiming her deepest thanks? Did she collapse into the nearest chair, fanning a lace handkerchief at her flushed cheeks, nearly overcome by the honor, the glory, the absolute wonderfulness of it all?

As Aunt Nellis was to think later in the privacy of her room—did pigs fly?

Christine did not immediately soar into high flights of ecstasy—or anywhere else, for that matter.

On the contrary, that ungrateful child, that viper at her bosom, that sullen, pouty-lipped changeling who couldn't possibly be her heretofore faultless niece, merely tossed her ivory cardboard voucher onto a plate of stale, half-eaten cucumber sandwiches and announced baldly, "Well, I sincerely hope you haven't pinned all your hopes and dreams on my becoming a roaring Sensation for you, Aunt Nellis, for I shan't do it. I hate London."

Nellis closed her eyes, hurt even as she had known she would be hurt. After leaving Hawk's Roost, the older woman had suffered gamely through nearly a week of stony silence from the girl without complaint, for she knew Christine believed herself to be suffering in the throes of her first blighted love.

Once the dam of silence had at last been broken, she had then patiently listened ad nauseum to Christine's complaints, her self-pitying whining, her sarcastic comments and general nastiness directed at the world at large and London society in particular.

She had lain awake nights, plotting ways to lure her niece to the modiste, the glovemaker, the milliner, and the bootmaker, only to fall into a fitful sleep and suffer nightmares that had her niece being presented to the king in last year's sprigged muslin.

She had cajoled and pleaded and made concession after concession, as a devoted, loving aunt should. But enough, by heaven, was enough and Aunt Nellis was not going to sit still for it anymore. The girl was actually thinking of turning down entry to Almack's!

It was sacrilege, that's what it was!

"You hate London, you hate London," her much-abused aunt retorted, finally losing her temper, and not much caring that her double chin was prone to wobble most unattractively when she allowed herself to become agitated. "Do you have any idea how ridiculous you sound, Christine? How childish? If you were a few years younger, I vow I would box your ears." She took two steps in her niece's direction. "As a matter of fact, I think I just might!"

Could Christine have heard aright? Threats of violence from a woman who had raised her voice in anger at her no more than three times in her memory, a woman who never so much as rapped her niece's knuckles? Clearly taken aback, Christine lifted her head to look up into her aunt's face. She expected to see anger. What she found there was despair.

"Oh, Aunt Nellis," she was stung into saying, "you have every right!" She jumped up to throw her arms around the woman, kissing her firmly on the cheek. "I've been horrid, haven't I? You have sacrificed so much, and I've been so wretchedly ungrateful, thinking only of myself. Can you ever forgive me?"

Aunt Nellis stood very still, trying to understand this latest development. Just as she was beginning to believe she had every right to be overset, the girl had jumped up and put her arms around her, agreeing with every word she had said. How was a woman to know how to deal with such an abrupt turn of events? It was terribly confusing.

"Yes, you have," she woodenly answered at last. One particular memory came to mind, unbidden, and she decided to give vent to it before holding it in did some terrible damage to her spleen. "Most especially last week at Lady Victoria's soiree, when you laughed at Lord Huxley as he was most kindly explaining the progress of the war to you and mistakenly placed Switzerland beside the Atlantic Ocean."

"Actually, Aunt, I believe he said Austria," Christine corrected, laughing a bit at the memory.

"Whatever, Christine. Please don't interrupt while I am trying to make a point. The man was mortified, and has been spreading rumors ever since that you are nothing but a mean-spirited bluestocking. You have been going out of your way to thwart me, Christine. I had such high hopes for this Season."

Christine stayed within her aunt's embrace. "I

know you had, Aunt. I did too, honestly I did, but that was before, before—"

"Before Lord Hawkhurst. Yes, my dear, I know. But have you ever stopped to consider that you are disappointing him as well as me? He wanted you to have a Season before you committed yourself to him. He explained that to me most thoroughly before we left Hawk's Roost. I was much impressed with his concern for you, even if I can't quite like the idea of your marrying the man."

Pulling away, Christine shook her head, the tears that were never far from the surface these days burning behind her eyes. "I am already committed to him, Aunt. I could never love another."

Aunt Nellis surreptitiously wiped at the tears that had gathered in the corners of her own eyes and plunged into what she was afraid would be dangerous waters. "I know that you feel that way now, Christine, but what about your feelings after you have learned why his lordship fled to the country all those years ago? You purposely avoid hearing anything against him. I have heard things since we've been here—not that I was indiscreet, for I wasn't, but merely steered the conversation in that direction once or twice—and I think you should be aware of what he did."

"*No!*" Christine cried, clapping her hands to her ears. "That is the very last thing I want to do. I refuse to listen to vicious gossip, doubtlessly twisted and turned every which way until it barely resembles the truth. Someday Vincent may tell me what happened, but in the meantime, I don't want to know. I have no interest in knowing. I've already told him that."

Aunt Nellis took a deep breath and shot off a verbal cannon across Christine's bow. It was time someone brought the child to her senses. "Then you don't care that a certain Mr. Belden has been invalided back from Spain and is bound to put in an appearance at Almack's tomorrow evening?"

Christine's head snapped back as if she had just been slapped. "Belden—Fletcher Belden?"

Aunt Nellis carefully inspected a slight dry area on the back of her hand. Obviously she had scored a flush hit. "Yes, Fletcher Belden. Quite a tragic figure, I'm told. Seems he went off with Wellington, hoping to get himself killed, but only succeeded in making a war hero of himself, mentioned in dispatches more than the weather." She looked up at her niece. "Or so I'm told."

"I hate—" Christine began, then stopped. Hadn't she quite worn that particular phrase to death? Besides, there might be a way she could turn this coincidence to her favor. Vincent wouldn't come to London because of Belden. What if she were introduced to the man, got to know him? Perhaps she could effect a reconciliation between these two troubled men. It would mean so much to Vincent.

"Yes, Christine?" her aunt prodded, seeing the intense look on her niece's face and wondering what the girl was thinking that had her looking more animated than she had in weeks. Aunt Nellis didn't dislike Lord Hawkhurst. It was impossible to dislike the man who had been, although strange, very kind to them in his own way, once he had gotten to know them.

She wasn't even put off by his scars, which weren't, in truth, all that awful. There were many very fine gentlemen in London at this very moment who had fared far worse in the war, losing arms and legs and eyes. No, the scars didn't bother Aunt Nellis. But the reason those scars were there—that was another matter entirely.

But what she liked least of all was his effect on Christine. He had not been what she'd had in mind when she had thought of a husband for her only niece. And after hearing what she had since coming to London, she had even begun to doubt her earlier good opinion of him, and remember more and more the way he had treated them that first night, trying to throw them back out into the cold to die.

What she had hoped for ever since Christine was born, and especially ever since their enforced stay at Hawk's Roost, was that Christine would prove to be a Success. Now she also prayed that Christine's pretty head would be so filled with beaux and parties and fancy balls that Vincent Mayhew would become nothing more than a silly, romantic memory of first love.

Yet, so far, Christine had proved extremely uncooperative. She had attended the parties her aunt had received invitations for, but she had not exactly gone out of her way to be congenial. As a matter of fact, if she were to be allowed to continue on in this same way for another few weeks, the Season would be well and truly ruined.

Vincent Mayhew would win through default.

That was why she had dared to mention Fletcher Belden. Christine would have to be on her best behavior and in her best looks to attract such a man. He was, from all accounts, a truly wonderful, decent man, a man worthy of someone as precious as Christine. He might not be the one to win her heart, but he could be the one to rescue her from her attachment to Hawkhurst, merely by telling her the truth about what had happened to his sister those many years ago.

She was sure Christine would listen to what Mr. Belden had to say, for then she would be able to satisfy her curiosity—which she would have been less than human not to have—without stooping to listening to gossip.

Aunt Nellis, her mind jumbled with all her convoluted thoughts and optimistic hopes, crossed her fingers behind her back and waited for her niece to speak.

Christine took a deep breath and exhaled slowly, a smile lighting her features and lightening her heavy heart. "I think I shall wear Vincent's pearls tomorrow night, Aunt Nellis. They should go quite nicely with my new gown, don't you think?"

"You'll be the most beautiful, sought-after young lady there, my dear," Aunt Nellis answered happily.

TWENTY

Christine stood up for her first waltz at Almack's the following evening, having first received the kind permission of one of the patronesses to take to the floor. She had seethed inwardly at the necessity for such foolishness when her aunt had told her of it, but then she shrugged her shoulders and allowed herself to be led across the room toward an imposing-looking dowager in a purple turban, saying, "Oh, well, it is their hall, isn't it, Sir Henry? I imagine we should humor them."

This potentially suicidal quip had her partner gushing that he believed her to be "a real right un," a sentiment Sir Henry Winchester repeated to his three very best friends once he had returned Christine safely to her aunt after the waltz was over. "Nothing die-away about that one," he added, "and light on her feet, too. I may decide to be in love with her, if she's got a good portion, of course."

"Of course," his friends seconded in unison, nodding solemnly for, although young, they were, after all, a practical bunch. Beauty would, in time, fade. Wit, especially in a woman, could grow tiring. But wealth, if handled carefully, was a joy forever.

In order to help their friend along in his quest to ascertain the financial eligibility of his prospective bride, each of the three gentlemen took to the floor with Christine in turn, an action she could only consider a mixed blessing. She was here to see and be seen, that much was true, so it would not do to be a wallflower, stuck in a corner with her aunt. However, she could be grateful to the young men and still regret their propensity for doing the majority of their dancing on her toes.

All four gentlemen had asked rather breathless, probing questions as to her financial expectations as they clomped through the steps of the reel and other rollicking romps, only thinly masking them in the guise of polite dance-floor conversation, so that Christine felt it only fair that she ask a few questions of her own in return.

As this sort of ungloved inquisition was rather out of the ordinary for a gentle female, the gentlemen reported back to each other that she must surely be a heretofore undiscovered heiress out to protect her own interests, and Sir Henry nearly had to pop his very best friend in the nose when that disloyal young man declared that he might just be thinking about stealing a march on his friend for the Heiress Denham's hand.

Society is strange as well as fickle—as well as lamentably easy to lead—and when other gentlemen present heard the four young men sparring over possession of the wealthy Miss

Christine Denham's hand, she suddenly became quite the most irresistible creature in the entire ballroom. How, they all asked themselves, had she passed through the Season unnoticed for so long?

"Her midnight dark hair is glorious, the widow's peak alluring past all words. And that perfect, heart-shaped face!" an impecunious baron was heard to say as he leered across the ballroom at an unsuspecting Christine.

"Sonnets should be written about those wide eyes, those rosebud lips! Odes, to the tip of her glorious nose! Fifty thousand a year, you say? I heard seventy-five," an aging baronet responded, wondering if his gout was up to a short whirl around the floor in a good cause.

"Very nice portion—not that it matters, for my heart is hers forevermore," vowed a colonel home on leave to bail his gambling-mad father out of the Fleet.

Sooner than a person could say "one hundred thousand at four percent" Christine found herself to be the center of masculine attention—and the target of many a nasty glare from the females in the room. Her aunt, nearly overcome with bliss, and for once deserted by her usual sense of impending doom, smiled and gurgled and allowed her outrageou pink and purple ostrich feathers to droop into her lemonade, shooed Christine back out onto the dance floor again and again, until the poor girl had to sneak away to the outdoor balcony to try to regain her breath.

She leaned against the railing, taking in deep gulps of the cool night air, wondering whether or not it would depress Aunt Nellis overmuch if she declared she had the headache and pleaded to return to Half Moon Street.

"I had begun to disbelieve in prayers ever being answered," a deep, velvety smooth voice came to her out of the darkness, "but you, my dear Miss Denham, have restored my faith. May I now pray that you will grace me with a few moments of your precious time before you go back inside to break more hearts?"

Christine whirled about, placing her back against the railing, to look into the darkened corner beside the full-length double window. "Who—who are you? How do you know my name?"

"Everyone knows your name, Miss Denham. It has been the only name worth hearing on anyone's lips all evening long. The beautiful Miss Christine Denham. The witty Miss Christine Denham. The very rich Miss Christine Denham."

"*Rich?*" Christine repeated this last statement in astonishment, still trying to make out her companion's figure in the shadows. Had she been doomed to forever have men hiding from her? "The beautiful Miss Denham I might chalk up to the thrill of the evening and a ridiculously expensive gown. The witty Miss Denham can only point out that it is terribly easy to be witty when your partners laugh at anything, including comments on the weather. The rich Miss Denham, however, is beyond me. Rich, you say?"

"*Very* rich," the man said, correcting her punctiliously and slowly advancing into the wedge of light cast outside by the chandeliers in the ballroom. "By that look of confusion on your *very* beautiful face, may I assume that the sudden acquisition of this wealth has caught you unprepared?"

"You might assume that," Christine agreed, just before getting her first real look at her companion. Her breath sucked in involuntarily and she knew her jaw was in danger of dropping to her knees. *What a glorious man!*

In height and build, he was very like her dearest Vincent, but there the similarity ended. This man was blond, his face deeply tanned by long exposure to the sun. When he smiled, as he was doing now, the skin around his clear gray eyes crinkled engagingly and a slashing dimple appeared in his right cheek. He was impeccably dressed in the fashion dictated by the patronesses, but his blue coat was subdued, and fit him as if he had been molded into it. He was, in a word, magnificent! And he was looking at her as if he believed she was magnificent as well.

"Who—who are you?" Christine heard herself ask, unable to believe he could have been inside the ballroom without her seeing him.

The man bowed deeply at the waist, then held out his hand so that she felt she had no choice but to offer hers in return. Lifting her hand to his lips, he placed a slightly longer than proper kiss on her fingertips, and then straightened. "My name is unimportant, for within a week we will address each other only as 'my dearest darling,' but I will tell you it anyway, for I am nothing if not polite. My name is Fletcher—Fletcher Belden. Will you do me the honor of becoming my wife?"

Fletcher Belden! Christine's head was reeling. This was the man who had cruelly, wantonly taken a horsewhip to her beloved Vincent? This was the sad, heartbroken soul who had taken himself off to war in the hope of spilling his blood all over the Spanish countryside? This was the man she was supposed to hate?

She withdrew her hand, her fingertips tingling where his lips had touched them. "I—I don't know quite what to say, Mr. Belden," she answered at last. "While I deeply appreciate your words, I must tell you that my affections are, um, otherwise engaged. I'm so sorry."

"Forget him!" Fletcher commanded with a dismissing sweep of his arm. "Heaven knows I have, and I have just heard of him. He doesn't deserve you."

It may have been dark on the balcony, but that didn't mean Christine could not see the twinkle in Belden's eyes. Tipping her head to one side, she sighed theatrically. "Alas, Mr. Belden, I cannot. You see, I love him. I love him quite desperately."

Fletcher shook his head sadly, then shrugged. "Well, no one can say I did not try, can they, Miss Denham? So, your heart belongs to another. All right, I can accept that. But does that mean we can't be friends?"

Now Christine laughed out loud. The man was insane! How could she possibly dislike him? "I would be honored to be your friend, Mr. Belden," she answered sincerely.

"Fletcher," he prompted, leaning down to tap her lightly on the chin. "Now, repeat after me: Flet-*cher*."

"Flet-*cher*," Christine parroted, not yet realizing that she was happy for the first time in weeks. "And I am *Chris*-tine," she continued, granting him the privilege of her Christian name.

"*Chris*-tine! Oh, I knew you were wonderful!" Fletcher congratulated her, holding out his arm so that she could lay her hand on his satin clad forearm. "Now all that's left is to see if you can follow my lead in the waltz, and we two shall become inseparable."

"Are you such a wonderful dancer?" Christine asked, allowing herself to be led back onto the dance floor.

"I am such a *terrible* dancer," he admitted with a grin, sweeping her into his arms. "I believe my dearest mama must have been frightened by a performing bear."

As they whirled about the room, his foot more often than not finding her abused toes, Christine forgot that she had planned to find Fletcher Belden here tonight—and then ruthlessly use him for her own purposes.

It was nearing midnight of another hard-fought day, but Vincent was still working, his left hand clutched around a tennis ball, his fingers pumping as he tried to squeeze the leather-covered object into submission. Beads of perspiration stood out against his forehead as he labored at his task, but he didn't care.

He was making progress, real progress. His arm was coming back from the dead. Christine would be so surprised, so pleased.

"Christine." As always, just the sound of her

name brought her face clearly to his mind's eye.

Putting the ball back into the dish on the table beside his chair, Vincent rose and walked over to his desk to pick up a calendar and check the date.

"Almack's has just reconvened for the Season, with all its dragons in their glory as they exercise the power of social life and death over this year's crop of hopeful misses," he mused aloud, remembering the frenetic excitement of Seasons past. "I wonder if Christine's aunt has been successful in procuring a voucher for her. She will be an instant sensation, I just know it."

Vincent dropped the calendar back onto the desktop, wondering why he felt so depressed. He had wanted Christine to go to London, to have a Season. Of course he had. Only then could she make an informed decision concerning their future. His future. She had given him so much, so very much. He owed her that.

He walked to the window and looked out over the moonlit garden, seeing the large, unbelievably ordinary ballroom at Almack's instead. The floor was empty save for Christine, dressed in filmy white draperies, his pearls about her slim neck. She was gliding gracefully across the floor on slippered feet, her kid-encased arms outstretched to meet her partner, a welcoming smile lighting her beautiful face.

A man appeared in the corner of Vincent's mental picture, tall and straight, and clearly anxious to have his arms around Christine as the musicians struck up a waltz. As they met in the center of the dance floor, Vincent could almost hear the violins begin to play, and he watched impotently as the man whirled Christine round and round the room, the two of them looking so happy, so unaware of their audience.

"*Arrrgghhhh!*"

Christine was in London, being toasted as the sensation of the Season, while he was here, hiding at Hawk's Roost, playing with tennis balls!

He must have been out of his mind to let her go! How could he have let her go? It had been a wonderful theory, and very unselfish of him, but it was also the most insane thing he had ever done.

"Lazarus!" he called out suddenly, all but running across the room to ring the bell that would summon the servant. "*Lazarus!* Pack my bags. We leave for London at first light!"

TWENTY-ONE

*W*ithin a week of their first meeting, Christine and Fletcher were accepted as a matched set wherever they went, and more than one enterprising gentleman had placed a wager at his club as to the date their engagement would be announced.

Everyone made much ado about the fact that Fletcher Belden, "that poor, poor man," was much deserving of the happiness he appeared to have found, while, secretly, frustrated mamas ground their teeth and rued the tragic loss of one of London's most eligible bachelors so early in the Season.

Christine was accepted everywhere, thanks to her youthful beauty, the surety that wherever she appeared Fletcher would not be far behind, and the general assumption that this Nobody from Nowhere was the heiress to a substantial fortune that had derived from a distant relative's shrewd international trade, West Indies shipping, or a gigantic diamond mine—depending on which of the many gossips one chose to believe.

Whatever it was, her wealth was at least three

generations from the shop which, of course, made it perfectly acceptable.

While Aunt Nellis went along from ball to picnic to rout party as chaperone, blissfully unaware of the gossip and believing that her niece had at last come to her senses and forgotten that strange, ill-starred Lord Hawkhurst, Christine and Fletcher were indulging themselves in a private game that had little to do with romance and a great deal to do with having some much-needed fun.

At least, that's what Christine believed.

She had quickly abandoned any thoughts of pumping Fletcher for information about the incident with Vincent, deciding once and for all that it was old news and best forgotten.

In time, with her at his side to love him, Vincent would forget the past, a past that included his obvious adoration of a beautiful woman named Arabella. Christine wasn't so altruistic that she wished to hear Vincent ever wax poetic about his lost love.

Possibly, when she was a happily married woman with grandchildren crawling about at her feet, she would indulge her husband in his reminiscences if he was of a mind to share them, but not until then. Her mind, her thoughts, her hopes, were all for the future.

What Christine did not know, but was soon to find out, was that Fletcher's mind was also on the future.

"Yes, your lordship, a masked ball. Lady Wexford is trying to bring them back into fashion, or so I heard from two gentlemen who were discussing it rather loudly last night outside White's," Lazarus said, setting the tea tray in front of his master. "It's planned for three days time from now, and half of London is invited."

Hawkhurst watched as the servant poured a cup of the hot liquid, absently making a steeple of his fingers as he sat among the shadows in a deep burgundy leather chair in the study of his Grosvenor Square mansion, the heavy velvet draperies shut tight against the afternoon sunlight.

He had been in town for over a week, entering the city after dusk in a closed, unmarked traveling carriage, to sneak into his mansion under the cover of darkness. The house had been in dust sheets ever since he had recovered sufficiently from his injuries to escape to Hawk's Roost over four years ago, and it had been a shock to his system to enter the dusty, stale-smelling structure and remember that the place had once been his uncle's pride and joy.

Lazarus and the small staff he had brought with him from Hawk's Roost had quickly set to work airing the earl's bedchamber, the kitchens, a few servants' rooms at the top of the house, and the small study at the rear of the first floor of the mansion. His lordship had needed no other rooms, for he did not plan to make his occupation of the place known and too much hustle and bustle would have the news broadcast throughout the *ton* in an instant.

Not willing to travel about the city personally, Vincent had been relying on Lazarus for news of Christine, news the servant had taken it upon himself to greatly dilute before presenting it to the man—especially when it came to the stories linking the young woman to Vincent Mayhew's greatest enemy, Fletcher Belden.

Lazarus had seen this action as a kindness to his master, a man he had begun to think of as a friend as well as an employer, so that Vincent only knew that Christine was experiencing a grand success in Society.

"A masquerade," Vincent mused now, absently accepting the cup of tea from the servant. "Oh, Lazarus, you know, I am sorely tempted to—but no, I cannot. I promised her this time on her own. It wouldn't be fair of me to interrupt her fun. I only want to be close to her, so that I might know she is all right. It was never my plan to intrude, and so I told her aunt."

Lazarus bit down hard on his knuckle, clearly caught up in a dilemma. Part of him wanted his lordship to remain happy in his ignorance, and another part of him wished for the earl to go after the heartless, fickle Miss Denham, sweep her into his arms, and carry her back to Hawk's Roost before it was too late. If his lordship were to be hurt again, it might be more than Lazarus could do to save him.

"You could wear a domino, your lordship," Lazarus suggested at last, his decision made. "That way nobody would know you, as everyone there will be rigged out in a costume of some sort."

"I would need a mask that covered my face completely," Vincent said thoughtfully. "No! I promised myself I would stay away, and that's just what I intend to do. There is more than a month to go before the Season draws to a close. Then I shall have you deliver an invitation to Hawk's Roost to the ladies. I shall have to wait, my friend, before I know my fate. This time I shan't rush my fences. Heaven knows the disaster I caused the last time."

Lazarus expelled his breath in an audible sigh of exasperation. Nevertheless, he tried again, his voice low and conspiratorial. "If you don't talk, don't say a word, she'd never be the wiser. Your arm is nearly well now, so that it won't give you away, and the mask would cover your face. Why, you could even *dance* with Miss Denham, and see for yourself that she is fine."

Temptation comes in many forms, but the thought of holding Christine in his arms was more than temptation—it was an irresistible lure. Setting down his cup, Vincent looked up at the servant. "I don't know, Lazarus," he began hesitantly, "it sounds innocent enough . . ."

Lazarus smiled, believing himself to have single-handedly saved his lordship's chance for happiness. "I walked out last evening with Mrs. Ernestine Flam, cook to Miss Nellis Denham. That woman would do anything for a pork pie, but all I wished from her was a little information. Miss Christine Denham is to attend the masked ball dressed as Queen Cleopatra of the Nile."

Vincent chuckled. "And Miss Nellis Denham's costume? The asp, I'm sure."

Lazarus wrinkled his brow, clearly puzzled at Hawkhurst's joke, but then quickly laughed along, not wishing to offend his lordship.

TWENTY-TWO

The massive ballroom was overflowing with gaily dressed peasant girls, their throats and ears dripping diamonds, courtly gentlemen in powdered wigs and sawdust-filled clocked hose, pitchfork toting devils with horns and leering grins, bosomy shepherd girls who would be hard-pressed to recognize a sheep, overaged, multipatched courtesans smelling of imported scent and domestic sweat, and more than half a dozen King Henry the Eighth's, at least two of whom needed no buckram padding to mimic the man's immense girth.

Lady Wexford had clearly outstripped even her own greatest expectations, for everyone who was anyone was in attendance at her masked ball this warm spring evening, including more than a few opportunistic gate-crashers who had managed to find their way onto the premises under the cover of costumes that would conceal their identities as long as they refrained from dipping their heads into the punch bowls and remembered not to drop their ''aitches'' when they spoke.

The air fairly crackled with excitement, as the

masks they wore freed the *ton* from the necessity of behaving themselves as they ought, and before the ball was halfway over more than a dozen innocent and not so innocent assignations had taken place in the privacy of Lady Wexford's ornamental gardens.

Lord Hawkhurst stood on the edge of the garden, able to see both the ballroom and the couples strolling arm and arm along the hedged walkways, a solitary figure enveloped neck to Hessians in a swirling black silk domino, his hair uncovered, his distinctive damning features hidden from the world behind a mask depicting a grinning, vacant-eyed skull that had been the only mask Lazarus could find that would cover his master's entire face.

"Look, Archy! 'ow gruesome! A death's 'ead!" a young woman dressed as Marie Antoinette might have looked had that poor beheaded queen had a few more pounds and a few less teeth, trilled to her partner, pointing straight at Vincent. "Oh, I think I might jist faint dead away."

Archy, a rather rotund gentleman clad in the costume of a court fool, complete with jangling bells on his toes, was not impressed. "Do, and I'll pull you into the bushes and tumble you anyway," he shot back roughly, pulling her toward the shrubbery. "You promised me a kiss. I haven't time for hartshorn and burnt feathers. We unmask at midnight and my wife will be looking for me."

"Oh, Archy! You gentry coves are *so* impatient!" Marie Antoinette teased, her eager hands already moving toward the buttons on his bright green breeches.

"And those same searching hands will be elbow-deep in his pockets before the night gets much older," Vincent remarked quietly to himself, wondering how he had ever thought he missed *ton* life as he made his way toward the ballroom.

But once inside the high-ceilinged room Lady Wexford had ordered decorated in mile after mile of pink, white, and golden yellow muslin, and enough flowers for a king's funeral, he quickly remembered that there were still things he liked about London. This penchant for divine absurdity was one of them.

He had been one of the brightest comets in the city during his years among the *ton*, part of a large circle of friends who favored the sporting life as well as the gentler side of Society. After a year spent in the Peninsula, he had returned to the metropolis ready for amusement and adventure and some lighthearted romantic dalliance, and he had found plenty to occupy his time.

It was only after Arabella Belden had made her debut that it had all changed, first for the better, and then—

Two gentlemen walked past, also clad in masks and dominos, one of them accidentally brushing up against Hawkhurst.

"So sorry, my fault entirely," the man murmured, not really looking at the person he was addressing.

"That's quite all right, Marcus," Vincent answered automatically, immediately recognizing the strapping redhead he had sparred with on several occasions at Gentleman Jackson's Boxing Salon. "You never could walk more than two feet without bumping into something."

Marcus Schillingham stopped in his tracks, leaning forward slightly as if this action would help him see the face behind the skull mask. "Damn these stupid things! Leave it to a woman to think up some silly nonsense to plague us. I sneezed a moment ago and nearly killed myself. Do I know you, friend? Your voice sounds so familiar, but I can't seem to place it."

Vincent searched his brain for an answer that would serve to fob off the man, but just then he spied a dark-haired beauty modestly yet alluringly clad in flowing white silk and a dozen or more gold bracelets appear ten feet in front of him just as the orchestra was striking up a waltz. Her midnight-black hair hung nearly to her waist, free of any restraint other than a thin golden band around her forehead, with the head of an asp rising above it. A small white mask circled her sky-blue eyes, but he knew her in an instant, even if Lazarus hadn't told him what costume she had chosen to wear.

Christine.

Quickly pressing Marcus's shoulder with one hand and mumbling something vague about catching up with him later in the card room, Vincent wasted no time in approaching Christine, bowing before her as he extended a hand toward the dance floor.

"Good luck to you, friend!" Marcus called after him bracingly, laughing as he moved to rejoin his companion, who was standing in the corner, openly leering down the bodice of a comely red-haired milkmaid.

"May I have the honor, Madame Queen?" Vincent asked, remembering to disguise his voice by dropping it a full octave. The grinning skull further distorted his words, so that even he didn't recognize his voice in the loud ballroom.

Christine was smiling up at him, clearly bemused by his horrific mask. Her eyes were full of mischief as she quickly consulted the dance card that was suspended from her wrist by a thin white ribbon. "You must be Death, I suppose, although you appear to be quite healthy. Let me see if I can locate you on my card, Sir Death. I have already promised dances to Romeo, and King Lear, and a man who I think believes he is an aged, graying Merlin but has only succeeded in looking as if he has been dumped head first into a flour barrel. No, I don't see any dead men here, although I do believe my last partner was tottering on the brink, for he has stumbled off somewhere, quite deserting me. I'm so sorry."

"Ah, fair Cleopatra," Vincent responded, taking her hand to lead her onto the floor, "what care you for dance cards? You are queen of all you survey, and may choose your own partners."

Christine tipped her head to one side, grinning impishly. "Yes, I am, aren't I? What a grand thought. But then why, Sir Death, I must ask, should this powerful queen deign to dance with you?"

"Because an asp, dear lady, has no feet," Vincent retorted, pulling her into his arms before

he exploded from the need to hold her. He turned
her neatly, effortlessly, as they swept into the first
full circle of the waltz.

And then the magic of the dance was on them
both, and there was no further need for words.

He cradled her slim body loosely, achingly
aware of her nearness, of her left hand placed on
his arm just above his elbow, of her right hand
nestled confidently against his palm. She was
more than a full head shorter than he, yet as he
whirled her about, the pure, violet scent of her skin
and hair wafted up to his nostrils as an invisible
fist squeezed shut deep inside him, reawakening a
hunger that had never really been fully satisfied.

Round and round they danced, their steps perfectly matched, their every movement one of grace
and beauty. Christine's white draperies flowed
beind her as she appeared to float an inch above
the ground, while Vincent's ebony silk domino bil-
lowed, exposing his black full evening dress, then
molded itself to his lean, muscular figure as he
stepped forward into another dizzying turn.

Christine was silent, staring up into his masked
face, and his tall frame bent only slightly toward
her, protectively, possessively, as he returned look
for look, his jaw tight, their gazes locked together
in wordless communication.

He was dying, but it was a most beautiful death.
He was living, for the first time in months, and life
had never been more sweet. The music was in his
head, in his heart, in his soul, and it was the most
beautiful music he had ever heard; an angel
chorus, played on golden harps. He wanted to

dance with Christine forever, hold her forever, look at her forever.

But nothing last forever, not happiness, not even pain, and certainly, not a waltz at Lady Wexford's masked ball. The musicians ended the dance with a flourish of violins and the dancers separated, each eager to find either a secluded spot to continue their conversations or another, more congenial partner.

Vincent and Christine stood quite still in the center of the rapidly clearing floor, still frozen in the graceful posture of the waltz, silently looking at each other, oblivious of the rest of the world.

Finally, her voice very small, Christine asked, "Who—who are you?"

He was tempted. He was so tempted. Even behind the safety of a mask, Christine seemed to know him. Surely this was a measure of their love for each other. Could he dare it? Could he chance it?

Yet could he bear to hold her, and then walk away?

Vincent raised his right hand to his face, taking hold of a bottom corner of his mask. "I'm—"

"Cleopatra! Ah, Cleo, my fatal darling! Have you forgotten that you have promised me this next dance? I hadn't known queens were so forgetful. I'm surprised you haven't misplaced a few pyramids by now."

Vincent's hand stilled in the act of removing his mask. That voice. He knew that voice. It was just that the last time he had heard it, the voice had been full of agony, cursing him, condemning him to pain, and degradation, and a lifetime of guilt. Now that voice was light, carefree, and addressing Christine in a very personal, very knowing way.

Christine stiffened visibly, a frown marring her smooth features at the untimely interruption, but her expression soon cleared and she turned away from Vincent to say, "Mark Antony, you have come! Allow me to introduce to you the mysterious Sir Death, someone we all must face at one time or another. We have just been dancing together, death and I. Sir Death, may I present the Roman upstart—" she began, turning back to where Vincent had stood only a moment earlier. "Sir Death?"

Slowly, Christine turned to Fletcher Belden, her hands spread wide, her expression puzzled and somewhat sad. "Now isn't that the oddest thing? He's gone."

"You're strangely silent, Christine. Are you tired? We could go back inside."

Christine shook her head and continued walking down the bricked path. It was hard to believe Lady Wexford could have such an extensive garden, here in the heart of Mayfair, and she had asked Fletcher to escort her outside so that she could take a closer look at it. "I'm not tired, really. I just feel rather—quiet. Do you understand?"

Fletcher pulled her hand more fully through the crook of his arm, watching as her thin shawl slipped from her shoulder. The look in his eyes, had she seen it, would have had her scurrying back to the safety of the ballroom.

"I understand, Christine," he answered softly,

leading her toward a curved stone bench that sat back from the path beneath a group of small, ornamental trees. "Let's sit here a moment, and we can be quiet together."

They sat side by side for some minutes, lost in their own thoughts, before Fletcher spoke again. "We've enjoyed ourselves, being together like this, haven't we, Christine?"

She turned her head to smile up at him, for she liked him very much. "You know we have, Fletcher. You're the best friend I've had since coming to London. The only friend, for that matter. I don't know how I would have gotten through these last weeks without you."

Fletcher's gaze was warm, his smile hinting of his happiness. "You know, I hated the thought of coming back to town. Really hated it. I—I had a rather bad experience here once, one I'd rather put behind me. I had feared the memories would all come rushing back once I—but that doesn't matter anymore. That first night, when I saw you across the ballroom floor, my mind became a merciful blank. I think I've lived my entire life waiting for you to come along."

Christine's heart suddenly leapt into her throat, choking her. "Fletcher, I—"

"No," he cut her off, holding up his hand to press his fingertips against her lips. "Please, Christine, don't say anything. Don't say a word, please, until I'm finished. I want to get this just right."

Her eyes burning with unshed tears, Christine reluctantly nodded her agreement.

He removed his fingers, only to begin lightly

stroking the side of her face. "I know you thought I was joking, but I meant it that first night. I want to marry you. Everything that's happened since then has only made me more sure. I love you, Christine. I can make you happy. Please—please marry me."

He could see them in the distance, sitting together, speaking earnestly, their voices near whispers that he could not overhear. His hands clenched into fists.

It wasn't fair. Not her. Not him. Dear God, not him. It wasn't fair!

When Christine's hand came up to cup Fletcher's cheek, and his head lowered so that their lips met, Vincent groaned aloud, then melted back into the night.

TWENTY-THREE

"**G**ood lord, I do believe I've just been insulted," Fletcher remarked wryly once the short kiss was over. "Father would be so disappointed in his son."

"Insulted?" Christine repeated in confusion, sitting back and folding her hands in her lap. She had kissed him impulsively, to quiet his words before he could continue, and to show him that she was very fond of him.

Fletcher smiled, although his expression remained crestfallen. "That kiss, Christine. It was the sort you would give your brother, or a kind elderly uncle. I've been kissed a time or two before, you see, and I've learned to recognize the difference. You really do love that other man, don't you? Even worse, you were totally unaware that I've been falling more madly, passionately in love with you each day over these last two weeks. It's enough to make a man doubt his own importance."

Christine blinked, trying not to embarrass him with her tears. She felt so sorry for him, for she had grown fond of him. "You're a wonderful man," she told him quickly. "Any woman would be fortunate to have you love her. It's just . . . it's just that—"

Fletcher cut her off. "Yes, I know. It's just that you're 'quite desperately' in love with someone else. I had assumed it was some fuzzy-cheeked squire's son who lives near Manderley, and no real competition for a sophisticated man of the world like myself. Overweeningly arrogant, wasn't I? I didn't even want to know his name before, but now I find myself overcome with curiosity. Tell me who he is, Christine, for I would dearly love to do him an injury."

Looking down at the ground, hiding the swift pain his words evoked, Christine said simply, "You already have, Fletcher. Done him an injury, that is. The man I love is the Earl of Hawkhurst, Vincent Mayhew."

Christine had been sure Fletcher's reaction would be one of anger, outrage, even disgust, and she was prepared to defend Vincent to him. But it was none of these. Fletcher's complexion paled visibly, his strong jaw clenched, and he slowly bowed his head.

"Vincent," he said slowly at last, shaking his head, his tone one of wonderment. "Dear God, so there is justice in this world after all."

"You can't go, your lordship! Please reconsider. He might kill you this time."

Vincent carefully removed his servant's hand from the sleeve of his jacket. He had been sitting alone in his study for two hours, thinking of what to do next. Now his course was clear. "Why should he kill me, Lazarus? He has everything he wants now. His revenge is perfect."

"But then, why go at all?" Lazarus was distraught. It was his fault that his master was so upset, his and Christine Denham's. He never should have pushed him into attending that masquerade.

Throwing his black silk cloak around his shoulders, Hawkhurst headed for the front door of his mansion. "Because I need to hear it from his own lips, my friend. I need to know if he really loves her or if he is only doing this to hurt me. I can't let Christine become a part of his revenge."

Lazarus watched helplessly as the earl slammed out into the night, uncaring if anyone saw him. "Women!" he declared, shaking his head. "There's never been a true one yet, to my way of thinking."

Fletcher Belden sat alone in the small book-lined room that served as his study. His town house had been closed during the time he had been away playing at war with Wellington, and the servants had still not been able to completely banish the musty smell of dust and damp, not that he noticed that fact at this moment.

It was nearly three in the morning, long past the hour of rational thinking if a person had been drinking heavily since soon after midnight, but Fletcher's mind had remained disgustingly clear.

Vincent.

"I believe this must be what the poets like to call irony," he mused aloud, peering into his half-filled brandy snifter as if he would see the answers to all the world's macabre, twisted jokes floating there in the amber liquid. "Or is that poetic justice? I can't remember."

"It's Greek tragedy, and badly done at that. You should have paid stricter attention in class, Fletcher, rather than spending all your time thinking up ways to get the innkeeper's daughter to meet you after dark at the King's College Cricket Ground."

"*Vincent!*" Fletcher cried out, leaping to his feet so that the snifter flew unheeded from his hand, to crash on the tile hearth. He looked down at the mess stupidly, then noticed that his legs were splattered with the spilled liquid. Without looking up he said, "That was the last of a damned good brandy, old fellow—and it hasn't done my breeches a world of good, either."

When Hawkhurst didn't comment, he straightened and looked about the room, trying to locate his old friend. "You're here to kill me, I imagine," he remarked in a calm voice, at last making out a dark figure near an open window and idly wondering why he had not immediately noticed the cool evening breeze that was now stirring the sheer curtains. Obviously, Vincent had decided to bypass the front door.

The shadow moved slightly, but remained silent as the tension grew in the dark room.

"I had already planned to avail you of my person tomorrow—today, in fact, as it is nearly dawn— but then I thought you were still buried at Hawk's Roost. Have you been in town long? No matter, I'm sure you don't want me taking up precious time with idle chatter. But do allow me to thank you for saving me the journey. Pistols, Vincent?

I'd rather not have to dance about with a sword, huffing and puffing inelegantly until you could find a way to run me through."

"I'm not here to fight with you, Fletcher," Vincent told him, taking another step into the light cast by the fire in the grate. "I've just come to inquire as to your intentions for Miss Christine Denham. Are they honorable?"

Fletcher stepped back a pace, his expression wry, yet strangely sad. Obviously, he had not anticipated this question. "So noble, Vincent. And, alas, so very much in character. Have you sprouted wings yet? I believe angels have hulking white wings, which would explain why you wear that cloak.

"Must be deuced wearying, lugging the feathery things about everywhere, not to mention the inelegance of molting twice a year. You remind me, painfully, of the way you stood so straight and tall, taking everything I could give you, as I wielded that god-awful horsewhip. You always were the better of the two of us. My God, if I weren't feeling so damned guilty already I could almost lie to you and tell you that Christine and I are deeply in love and plan to marry as soon as possible."

Fletcher now had a clear sight of Vincent, or at least as clear as it could be, for the man remained half hidden inside the hooded black domino. "You don't love her?" Hawkhurst shot back angrily. "Then you were taking advantage of her tonight! God! I *could* kill you for that!"

Pressing his fingertips against his forehead, Fletcher slowly shook his head, laughing softly. "Still so passionate, Vincent? How can such an otherwise intelligent man be so ignorant when it comes to women? And now it would appear you have taken to hiding behind hedges, peeking at someone else's private moments."

"I saw you together in the gardens, yes," Vincent admitted, just the mention of that scene nearly inciting him to riot. "You were kissing her."

"Wrong, Vincent. I was proposing to her. The lady turned me down, old friend, turned me down flat. Imagine that—me, the man who has prided himself on being irresistible since he was out of short coats. It seems she'd rather wed a stubborn recluse who keeps trying to send her away."

Vincent took a few more steps, then collapsed his tall frame into the closest chair, sighing audibly. "My God, my God," he said, nearly overcome. "I thought I had lost her. Oh, Christine!"

Fletcher crossed to the drinks table and poured two generous portions of port, then held one out to Vincent. "Rather boggles the mind, don't it? Here, drink this. You've got another shock coming, and after hearing what I've got to say you might just reconsider and decide putting a period to my existence is exactly what you do want. If I can get you drunk enough, your aim might suffer."

Vincent took the glass automatically, still trying to recover his composure. He had been so sure, so very sure, that he had lost Christine forever. He looked up at Fletcher. "She allowed your kiss. Why would she have done that?"

"Ah, we're still in the garden, are we?" Fletcher reflected, draining the contents of his own glass.

"So, you were witness to only a small part of my shame, were you? You shouldn't have run off, but stayed, to watch while the lady cut my legs out from under me. Not that Christine wasn't kind, for she was, which was why she kissed me. Rather like tossing a bone to a toothless dog, but I'm sure she didn't see it that way. But, to tell the truth, I'm rather glad that I was allowed to fall on my face without an audience. You're a lucky man, Vincent. I hope you know that."

"I know that," Vincent answered. ' I also know that I don't deserve her."

Fletcher pulled an armless chair over to face Vincent, turning it about so that he could straddle it. "Yes, we're back to that. I thought we would be. Your face—how is it? I can't really see you with that damned hood covering you. And your arm? You know, I thought I had killed you when you finally raised your arm to shield your face and the whip cut into your underarm. So much blood! Just like Arabella. I drank for three solid days, trying to forget what you looked like when I was done with you. Damn near five years—wasted. God, Vincent, how I've missed you!"

Reaching up his left hand, Vincent pushed the hood from his head. "The arm's fine, at last, and I'm not prettier than you anymore, if that's what you're worried about," he said, amazed at how very good he was feeling, just to be in the same room with Fletcher. They had been so close, closer than most brothers. It was almost like the old days, except— "You have something to tell me, Fletcher?"

Fletcher began rhythmically hitting the heel of

his hand against the wooden back of the chair. "Yes, Vincent, I do. If I drank for three days after beating you, I crawled into a bottle for damn near a week when I found out what I am about to tell you, then went off to Spain, doing my damndest to get myself killed. I couldn't face you, not then. When that didn't work, I came back here to throw myself on your mercy, even let you do the job the Frenchies couldn't." He shrugged his shoulders apologetically. "My intentions were good, but I'm afraid I got sidetracked." .

"Christine," Vincent said, oddly pleased to see the quick flash of pain in the other man's eyes.

"Christine," Fletcher agreed solemnly, then seemed to recover, flashing a grin. "I can't be sure, poor student that I was, but I believe it was Otway who said, 'Who lost Mark Antony the world? —A woman!' I knew I should have gone to that blasted masquerade as Robin Hood. Christine would have made a fetching Maid Marion."

There was silence in the room for some minutes, as one man reflected on his good fortune and the other rued his missed chance for happiness. As the clock struck the hour of four, Vincent asked, "What made you lose yourself in drink for a week? You haven't said."

Fletcher looked up, a tortured amusement lighting his blond good looks. "Noticed that, did you? I guess I'm still trying not to say it. But she was m'sister, you know, and once I say the words, they'll hang between us, where both of us can see them. I thought I was ready to let that happen, but now I'm not so sure. Yet you more than anyone deserve to know the truth."

Vincent was confused, and voiced his confusion. "You're talking about Arabella? What more is there to say? I tried to rush her into marriage and she wasn't ready for it, even if she had accepted my ring. The last night, when I kissed her, when I let my love for her overtake my better judgment and dared to make her surrender to my will, I frightened her more than I knew. It was all there, in the notes she left behind."

Fletcher shook his head. "No, it wasn't. Both of us thought so, but it wasn't. The real truth was in her diary. I found it about a month after her funeral. My sister, Arabella, sweet, innocent Arabella, was pregnant."

"Pregnant!" Vincent shot out of the chair, running a hand distractedly through his hair. "But—but, that's impossible! Fletcher, I swear to you, I never—"

"I know that!" Fletcher interjected quickly, rising to lay his hands on his friend's shoulders. "It was someone else. A French prisoner of war given the freedom of our village, blast the man, for he'd been sent back to France before I could search him out and kill him."

"A Frenchman?" Vincent heard a roaring in his ears. It was all so unbelievable. "But her notes—the ones she wrote both of us before she cut her wrists—in those she said she couldn't face the physical side of marriage and was taking the only way out she could think of that would save everyone pain. I had thought it was because I had— But she had given me every indication that she wanted me as much as I wanted her. It was just at the last minute, when she began to cry, that I realized that

I had frightened her. I was going to let her break our betrothal, was about to come to this house to tell her so, when you came to me to say that she was dead. Oh my God! How did this happen?"

Fletcher left his friend standing, stunned, in the middle of the room and went to refill their glasses. "It's not a pretty story, but it's only fair that you hear it all. Here, drink this," he said, returning to press the glass into Vincent's hand. "Before this night is through we're both going to rue the fact that spirits were ever invented. Do you remember, Vincent—I hardly ever drink."

As dawn broke over London, Fletcher told Vincent the whole story. His younger sister had been the light of his life, and he had kept her safely secluded in the country after their parents died, until he thought she was ready to take London by storm. She had come to town with him most willingly, a quiet, biddable child, too angelic, too beautiful to be mere flesh and blood, and Vincent had taken one look at her and fallen deeply in love.

Fletcher had been overjoyed. His best friend and his only sister; it was a perfect match! Arabella had readily agreed to the engagement, and begged Fletcher to allow an immediate wedding.

"She knew she was pregnant, of course, old friend," Fletcher said, shaking his head, "and planned to let you believe you were the father. She was distraught, knowing I'd be devastated if I found out what she had done. I think it must have unhinged her.

"Looking back on it, and believe me, in the years since I found that diary I've had ample time for thinking back on everything that happened, I've decided she purposely set out to seduce you that last night, just to make sure there would be no question that you were the father. She just couldn't go through with it."

"She never loved me," Vincent said, as if to himself. "All this time, and she never really loved me."

"She loved that bastard frog," Fletcher spat, hurling his empty glass into the dying fire, "and he left her to deal with her shame alone. But I think she did love you, at least a little. Loved you enough that she could not go on deceiving you. I only wish she could have told the truth in her notes, but she protected that bastard to the end, not realizing that you and I—the whole world—would think the worst."

"Nobody can ever know of this," Vincent declared vehemently, at last coming out of his reverie. "I'll go on, taking the blame for her death. I loved Arabella. I will never allow her name to be dragged through the mire, Fletcher. I promise you that!"

There were tears in Fletcher's expressive gray eyes. "I don't deserve that, old friend, although I must admit I half expected it. As I said, you always were the noble one. But think of it, Vincent; between us, Arabella and I damn near ruined your life. I can't let you carry my burden any longer. It wouldn't be fair."

"As long as I know the truth, it doesn't matter what anyone else thinks of me," Vincent told him, idly fingering the scars he knew so well. He had finally gotten up the courage to face them in the mirror, and knew that they were no longer the horror he remembered, but that didn't mean he was ready to show them to the world. "I've quite lost my taste for London anyway."

"And Christine?" Fletcher prodded. "You would condemn her to hide with you in the country forever? She blossoms in London, old friend. And she loves you—'quite desperately.' If she were on my arm, I could face the devil himself, let alone the dragons of Society."

"Memories fade, Fletcher, but not these scars. They'd be a constant reminder, everywhere I went. I can't subject Christine to that."

Fletcher spoke quietly, his eyes intent on Vincent's altered but still handsome face. "Not even if *I* were there too, standing beside my best friend?"

Vincent felt his throat growing tight. He had his life back, if he chose to take it. He had Christine, if he could dare to claim her. Maybe it was time to bury the past, and get on with the business of living.

TWENTY-FOUR

There was mist everywhere, ghostly pale, and swirling, moving around her knees as, dressed in an unearthly gown of trailing white gossamer, Christine moved across a wide expanse of nothingness. She could see her legs moving, but could not feel the earth beneath her feet. Her hair, unbound, was blowing softly about her in a gentle breeze that was neither warm nor cold, but simply there, a part of the scene.

Brushing a stray wisp of hair from her eyes, she looked about her, trying to understand where she was, what was happening to her. But there was nothing to see. She was alone in the middle of a vast, empty world. Yet she felt no fear—only expectation.

Christine was dreaming. Of course she was dreaming, she told herself, but she had no desire to shake her mind back into wakefulness, back to awareness, back to reality. She was here for a reason, to work out some great puzzle she hadn't known had been set out for her.

It was so strange how in dreams a person could see themselves, watch themselves, and still be themselves; remaining somewhere else, off in the floating distance, a very partial observer of their own fate.

Christine watched as she tipped her head to one side, as if listening to something, perhaps music. She watched herself turn, holding her skirts wide gracefully as she began to run, floating through the clinging mist, obviously eager to go someplace, be someplace, see some one.

Yes, that was it. Someone was waiting for her, watching for her, calling her to him. *Him.* Of course, it had to be a man. Christine could feel her heart pounding in expectation. He was here! He was waiting for her.

She watched the dream Christine running, her ebony hair streaming behind her, a smile lighting her face, happy tears wetting her cheeks.

At last, in the distance, a man appeared. He was wearing a flowing black silk cloak that molded itself to his tall body as the breeze became a whirlwind. His arms were flung wide in welcome, and Christine, her eyes squeezed tightly shut, urged her dream self to run faster, ever faster, so that she could hurl herself into his arms.

Vincent! she called loudly, silently, wordlessly, her voice resounding inside her head, his name a symphony of silent wonder, as she watched herself being enveloped inside the folds of that black cloak and felt his strong arms close around her, never to let her go.

Suddenly the dream Christine and the real Christine became one, as happens in dreams, and she dared to raise her head, to look at her love, to see him smiling down at her, hear him saying her name.

Her blood ran hot, then cold. It wasn't Vincent.

She was being held by a man with no face. A man with only a white, grinning skull, mocking her as he pushed her from him and melted back into the mist.

"*Sir Death!*" she screamed in her bedroom in Half Moon Street. "No, Sir Death! *Don't go!*"

"She loves you?"

Vincent kept his chin held high, allowing Lazarus to knot the cravat tightly about his throat. "Is that so astonishing, my friend?"

Lazarus felt his cheeks grow hot with embarrassment. "No, oh no, sir! Of course she loves you. You are a most wonderful person. Miss Christine would be a fool to do anything else."

Lowering his head once the servant had made his last careful adjustments to the snowy white linen, Hawkhurst gifted Lazarus with a mocking smile. "Don't overdo the praise, Lazarus. You might strain yourself. Now, fetch me my cloak, if you please. I don't wish to be more than fashionably late."

Lazarus scurried to do his master's bidding. "You're really going to do it? You're really going to go to the ball, like Mr. Belden said? Aren't you afraid?"

Vincent bent down slightly so that Lazarus could place the black silk cloak around his shoulders. "I'm more frightened now than at any time in my life, my friend," he admitted honestly.

"Of what people will say," the servant concluded, nodding his head.

"Of what Christine will say," Hawkhurst corrected feelingly, heading for the door. "Hers, my good friend, is the only opinion that matters."

"I still say you should be home in bed. You've obviously been trotting too hard, out every night to heaven only knows what hour with Mr. Belden. Much as I like the man, I think he should know better. You're very delicate, you know. You take after me, and I was always most delicate."

Christine shifted herself slightly on the cracked leather cushion of the rented carriage. She was so anxious for the evening to begin she could barely sit still. "It isn't Fletcher's fault, Aunt Nellis," she answered wearily. "Besides, it was only a dream. I'm sorry I woke you."

"Woke me? *Woke me!* You woke the whole household. I had to promise Mrs. Flam a Cornish hen all her own to keep her from walking out on the spot," Aunt Nellis retorted heatedly. "Screaming that way about death and dying and all sorts of nonsense. It took every pot and potion I had to get some bit of color into my cheeks tonight, Christine. That's how much you frightened me. I think I'll pull the rope and have the driver turn back to Half Moon Street. You shouldn't be out."

"No!" Christine cried, raising her hand to stop her aunt. She had to go to this ball tonight, she just had to. *He* might be there again. Sir Death! How could she have been so stupid? She had known immediately that he had been different, special.

Why hadn't it occurred to her that it had been Vincent? Why had it taken a dream to tell her?

And he had seen her with Fletcher Belden! How could she ever explain to him, make him understand? He had every right to hate her, to believe her to be the most fickle, hard-hearted female in nature! He had to come to her again, to let her explain. If he didn't, she'd know he had returned to Hawk's Roost, to brood, to curse her, to hide.

"Christine, let me go, please. You're hurting me," Aunt Nellis said quietly, clearly upset.

Christine blinked twice, then realized that she had taken hold of her aunt's wrist. "Oh, I'm sorry, Aunt," she apologized, taking her hand away. "It's just that this evening is so important. Fletcher promised he'd be there, and most particularly asked that I save him a waltz," she added, knowing Nellis was harboring hopes in that corner. "It wouldn't do to disappoint him, would it?"

Aunt Nellis was mollified, and the carriage continued to Portman Square.

Fletcher came up to her the moment she set foot in the ballroom, and no matter what she did, he refused to leave her side. While her Aunt Nellis beamed from her seat with the dowagers, Christine did her best to show him he really wasn't welcome, but the man refused to take the hint and go away. There was just no moving him.

He stood up with her for the first two waltzes, treading on her feet as was his custom, and then escorted her down to dinner over her protests that she wasn't hungry, keeping up an amusing monologue that would have had her laughing out loud if only she weren't so close to tears.

Her gaze barely left the main entrance to the ballroom as she held her breath, waiting, hoping, for Vincent to arrive. She knew she was poor company to the young men who led her out onto the dance floor, but she couldn't help herself, and at last simply begged off, saying that she had the headache.

But once she was seated away from the dance floor, fanning herself as she bit her lip and looked once more toward the door, Fletcher sat down beside her, appearing as if he was determined to support her in her agony.

"Headache, huh?" he asked conversationally, and a bit too happily, or so Christine thought. He sat back, crossing one leg over his other knee, obviously prepared to bear her company until the end of the evening.

Gritting her teeth behind a purely social smile, she gave up any pretense of politeness. "Fletcher," she whispered fiercely, "go away!"

"Oh, I'm hurt!" he responded, theatrically clutching at his chest. "Cut to the quick. I know you don't love me, but that doesn't mean we have to become strangers. Besides, you like me. You told me so yourself. It was just the other day—I remember it distinctly. You said, 'Fletcher, I like you.' I was very moved, I tell you. Very moved."

"Oh, stop it!" Christine ordered under her breath, smiling and nodding as Lady Wexford walked by, a look of censure on her horsey face. "Now look what you've done! The whole world and his wife will think we're engaged to be married."

"Really?" he questioned, raising his eyebrows speculatively. "Now, there's a thought. But I'm sure you said you were to marry Vincent Mayhew." He sat forward, looking toward the door. "Well, lookee there, if it isn't the earl himself, walking bold as brass into this very ballroom. Imagine that! I think I'll go say hello. Are you coming?"

Christine didn't move. She couldn't move. Her eyes shifted to look toward the doorway, then widened in disbelief. It *was* Vincent. He was standing just inside the doorway, dressed impeccably in black and white, his head uncovered and held high, not in daring, but as if he had every expectation of being welcomed with opened arms.

She placed her hand on Fletcher's arm, pulling him back down into the chair so that he let out his breath in a rush. "Hey!" he cried, removing her fingers. "You're crushing my sleeve, Christine. My valet would be grievously disappointed in you, I have to tell you."

"It's him," she breathed, still looking at Vincent.

Fletcher tilted his head and made a face. "Yes, I know. I've already said that. You didn't have to ruin my coat to tell me again, my dear."

"But—but you hate him," she stammered, then declared forcefully, "I won't let you hurt him, Fletcher. He's been hurt enough."

Now Fletcher took Christine's hand, gently pulling her to her feet. He was aware that the entire ballroom had gone very still, that every head was turned, looking from Vincent, to him, and then back again. He could almost smell their blood lust, just waiting to see what would happen.

"Darling girl," he said soothingly, slipping her hand through his arm, "I fear I have been unfair to you. Vincent and I have settled our differences, although I was tempted to hit him over the head, stuff him in a sack, and send him back to Hawk's Roost just so that I could have another try at winning your heart. But I knew it was useless."

Christine reluctantly drew her gaze away from Vincent, who was still standing just inside the doorway, looking in her direction. "Will he come to us, Fletcher? Is he really ready to come back?"

"I don't know, Christine," Fletcher answered truthfully. "He's been through a lot, one way or another. It wasn't easy getting him to agree to come here tonight. What do you say we meet him halfway?"

Holding tightly to Fletcher's arm, Christine allowed herself to be led across the empty floor, her vision narrowing until her world excluded everyone but Vincent. Her bottom lip began to tremble as he took one step, then two, into the ballroom, his handsome face speaking eloquently of his love for her, his scars a pale reminder of his past, but no longer a hindrance to his future.

They met in the middle of the floor, and Vincent's clear-eyed gaze shifted to Fletcher, who held out his hand in greeting.

Christine heard the two men speak, and although she couldn't understand what they were saying she knew that Fletcher was giving her over to Vincent, while at the same time letting everyone know that this man was his friend, now and forever. Her heart was beating too loudly to hear the actual words, her breath was tearing at her lungs, her vision clouded as tears welled in her shining sky-blue eyes, then spilled over onto her cheeks.

But she knew. They all knew.

She felt her hand being removed from Fletcher's arm and placed in Vincent's, the contact burning into her flesh. Turning on his heel, Fletcher walked away without turning back. The quiet that had been so deafening just a moment earlier was broken by guests beginning to chatter among themselves, disappointed to see that there wasn't going to be a scene, and the musicians quickly struck up a waltz.

Her head tipped back so that she could look up into his face, Christine reached inside herself to summon up a watery smile. "May I please have the honor of this dance, my lord?" she asked, moving into his open arms, her mouth forming a small circle of surprise as his left hand came up slowly to take hold of hers. Until that moment she hadn't realized that his arm was no longer hanging limply at his side. "Oh, Vincent," she said on a sigh, remembering how he had held her as they danced together at the masquerade.

"I've waited all my life for this, Christine," Vincent told her, his voice husky with emotion as he skillfully guided her into the first, sweeping movement of the dance.

Alone, in the center of the floor, they danced round and round, unaware that Nellis Denham was weeping softly into her handkerchief, overcome by the look of happiness on her niece's face; unaware that Fletcher Belden was standing on the perimeter of the dance floor, his handsome head held high, softly applauding; unaware that, together, they made a perfectly beautiful, perfectly wonderful couple.

TWENTY-FIVE

Hawk's Roost

Christine bent to lightly press her nose to the blood-red rose, the last bloom of summer, a beautiful flower just like the ones Vincent had brought to her the morning after their marriage.

It was fully dark, hours past the time he usually arrived home from his frequent visits to London, where he had taken up his seat in the House of Lords, but she wasn't worried. He would be home soon, he always came home to her. She would have gone with him, as she often did, if it weren't for the fact that she was carrying their first child and Aunt Nellis and Lazarus both had forbade the trip.

She turned to walk down the path leading back to the house, dressed in the white silk dressing gown that covered the sheer, lacy nightgown Vincent always asserted was his particular favorite— a sentiment he usually voiced just before ridding her of the gown and pressing her back against the soft pillows of their bed.

She looked up as she heard a slight noise, having

been concentrating her gaze on making her way over the moss-covered bricks in the darkness, and saw a masculine shape at the end of the path.

"Vincent?" she asked, knowing the answer, and she quickened her pace, her arms held wide. "I've been waiting for you, darling."

He stepped out of the shadow of the trees, his riding cloak still swinging around his knees, his head uncovered, and moved into the light of a full moon. "I'm here, Christine. I'll always be here."

He moved toward her, her beloved Vincent of the moonlight, and she ran to the heaven of his arms.

There's an epidemic with 27 million victims. And no visible symptoms.

It's an epidemic of people who can't read.

Believe it or not, 27 million Americans are functionally illiterate, about one adult in five.

The solution to this problem is you... when you join the fight against illiteracy. So call the Coalition for Literacy at toll-free **1-800-228-8813** and volunteer.

Volunteer Against Illiteracy. The only degree you need is a degree of caring.